DARK WATER

A WWI SEAFARING TALE

CHRIS SPECK

ISBN: 978-1-0687183-1-1

The *Kestrel* is a steam trawler built by Welton and Gemmell of Beverley in 1891 for the Humber Steam Trawling Company. She was floated down the river from the shipyard to Kingston Upon Hull where the engineering firm of Amos and Dunstan fitted her with a compound steam engine and one single boiler. Unlike the box fleets of smacks with their big flappy sails that fished together, she's a single boater, meaning that she'll go out trawling in the waters of the North Sea alone until the skipper's satisfied that she's full, and then they'll head home.

She sits tied to one of the big cleats in St Andrews Dock, Hull, with her engine as cold as stone and the fishroom below hollow. There's the smell of soap from where the scrubbers washed down the boards that separate the fish when it's been caught and stacked.

The *Kestrel* should be out on the waves catching slippery cod and haddock. She should be making the Humber Steam Trawling Company a killing like she has done for the best part of twenty-five years and yet, here she is in dock without a crew.

There's a war on. They say it will be over before summer. The Kaiser has marched his army into France and the British have gone off to stop him getting any further. It's not just the army who've been mobilized. In August 1914, the government passed the Defence of the Realm Act which meant they could requisition any vessel they fancied. The Humber Steam Trawling Company has lost the use of a good many of their best ships already, they have been turned into mine sweepers or scouts, but not the *Kestrel*. The engine is well past its best, the cylinders need replacing, the boiler is cracked, she needs a refit and a good paint job and the funnel is caked with soot and black with age. She made two trips in September to land fish before Skipper Reed decided that he couldn't ignore the war any longer, and he signed up along with most of the crew.

There may be a war in Europe, but people still need to eat, and with less fishermen out in the sea, the price has not been as high for a good long while. There's life in the *Kestrel* yet, and she's worth perhaps another twenty years. That's why the Humber Steam Trawling Company wants her at sea again, war or not, there's still money to be made.

Mr Keel takes a sip on his whiskey. He doesn't drink ordinarily, understand, his father used to say that it dulls the head in business, but he can't afford to get this wrong. Skipper Williams might think him effeminate or untrustworthy if he doesn't have one. He sits opposite the fire in one of the large, expensive terraces on the Boulevard just north of St Andrew's Dock. These ones have servant's quarters in the attic, and are the homes of men who made, or continue to make, a great deal of money from the sea.

In front of him, in a red leather armchair, sits a thin old man with cropped white hair. He has a white moustache and wrinkled skin that looks like it's been made from leather. This is Skipper Williams, the Old Fox, a legend amongst the Hull fishing community for his knowledge, guile, and the meanness of his spirit. He has commanded vessels for the last forty years out of this port, and there is not another soul perhaps who knows the North Sea better than he does—if only he were still young enough to sail.

Mr Keel works for the Humber Steam Trawling Company, primarily as a commissioner or a ship's husband, that means that he makes sure the boats are ready to sail with all the provisions they need and a crew as well. This is why he is here.

"You know, Skipper Williams, I heard there was even an advert in the paper a week or so back. It read 'ladies' petticoats wanted' and underneath 'for those men who refused to enlist

3

for the glorious war effort'. What do you make of that?" The old man has paper thin eyelids and bony hands. On the back of his leather armchair is an English blue cat. She has plush, well-kept fur and mean yellow eyes.

"If I were a lad, I'd be first in the queue," says Skipper Williams. His voice is croaky with age but there is steel within.

"Who'll catch the fish if all the men are off at war? Who's to man the trawlers? What will we eat?"

"You mean how are you and your company going to keep your cash till bells ringing?" Skipper Williams sees things as they really are. You don't get to seventy-four without a good understanding of the world. Mr Keel sets his glass down on the table in front of them and picks up the letter he has brought for the old skipper.

"We have a proposition for you, Mr Williams," says Keel with his smooth and clean face. He's part of the new generation of men that know all about the sea and boats but have never been out there. "There's a trawler we would very much like you to command, it's one of our most dependable vessels, called the *Kestrel*." The old man's face does not change. For the last three years he's sat in this huge house on the Boulevard with his daughter fussing round him like he was a fool ready to die. The blue short haired cat slinks down onto the Skipper's shoulder and then into his lap, she rubs her head into his rough hand.

"The *Kestrel*?" he asks, then narrows his eyes in thought. The *Kestrel* is well past its best and small. "She's twenty-five years old," he whispers, "she's a bloody rust bucket as it is."

"Skipper John Reed didn't seem to think so, and if he hadn't joined up for the war effort himself, he'd be out there now." The *Kestrel* is made of iron, steam trawlers these days are made with steel.

"I'm seventy-four," says Williams.

"I'm aware of that," answers Mr Keel.

"You'd trust me with the command of a vessel, in time of

war, at my age?" Williams is not really asking—he's far too old and knowledgeable to do that. This line is meant to make Mr Keel feel stupid and question his judgement.

"That's why my superiors sent me here, Skipper Williams."

"Is there nobody else to captain it?"

"No. There've been so many ships requisitioned already and their crews too, then there are all the trawlermen who joined up. We've nobody left. If you want to do something for King and Country, Skipper Williams, you can do what you've always done, you can command lads and you can fish." The blue cat purrs under the old Skipper's touch as she rubs her ears against his thumb. "It would be one last time, Skipper. You'd be paid well." Williams takes a deep breath. It's not as simple as just sailing out to sea, not at the moment.

"From what I've heard, the Germans have mined every inch of the North Sea." This is the truth. In August last year, the Kaiserliche Marine began laying mines around the East Coast, and just a few days after war was declared, one of these same mines blew up *HMS Amphion*, a three thousand tonne scout-cruiser. They are huge, spiked balls that hang just below the water's surface and their indifference will see them sink battle ships or fishing boats alike.

"Minesweepers are on it night and day," says Mr Keel, "you must have heard, they sweep huge paths between ports and right up to Scotland. That's what they've requisitioned all our trawlers for." Williams knows this. In the Manchester Street ale house, there's a lad who works one of these mine sweepers. He explained how it works, two refitted trawlers sailing parallel drag a line between them to lift the mines. He was half cut when he explained how they float the mines away and shoot them with rifles to blow them up. Skipper Williams does not do charity, but he made sure the lad had enough to get another few pints in him.

"It's like pissing in the wind," says Williams. "They'll be a thousand of them things in the North Sea." Mr Keel does not like to argue with this old seaman that he needs.

"If you keep to those lanes, skipper, you and the boat will be fine." The old man gives a half-hearted snarl.

"When?" he asks.

"Monday week."

"Tell me about the crew." Mr Keel gives a nervous smile. "Well, we're still gathering them, as I explained the pool of talent we have is not as big as it normally is."

"Who've you got?"

"First mate is a man called John Grace. A Scouser. He's got a face like a dog chewing a wasp, but he gets the job done."

"He's a miserable sod, and he's no lad. I sailed with him ten years ago and he was past it then."

"A good worker all the same and trustworthy too," Skipper Williams nods. Grace is all that.

"The Woods lad, as well. He's to be the bosun."

"Which one?"

"The youngest."

"Harold?"

"I believe Harold was lost with his father."

"Do you mean Tommy?"

"Thomas Woods, aye. He's agreed to act as bosun." Skipper Williams gives a snarl from the side of his mouth:

"The youngest Woods lad is lame."

"He can walk as well as anyone and he knows his boats, and his fishing. He's from a good family."

"He can sail, but he's any bloody skipper's final choice. Better not to have him on board than for him to mess up the job for others. I've heard he carries bad luck with him as well." Williams tuts and the blue cat looks up at him with nervous, yellow eyes. Tommy Woods really is known for being unlucky and skippers won't take him on a long haul. "He'll be washed overboard in a swell," grumbles Skipper Williams, "then who'll do his work?" Mr Keel blinks back at the skipper. Sometimes the best way to answer a question is not to answer it at all. "Who else?" asks Williams.

"Eric Cooper, deckhand and trimmer." Cooper is a five-foot coal worker who stinks. Skipper Williams knows him with his mucky paperboy style cap pulled low over his eyes.

"He's not had a bloody wash for ten years."

"Cooper has a reputation for working hard, Skipper." This is true.

"Who else?"

"Peter Everett."

"Who's he?"

"The engineer." The name is not familiar to the skipper but he will be educated if that's his skill. "We have a cook, Stout." Williams is aware of this character, an unpleasant fat man who is work-shy at best.

"Is that it so far?"

"Yes," answers Keel.

"You have John Grace, the lame Woods lad, a trimmer who hasn't bathed since he was a child, some engineer, and a greasy cook, and me. Is that it?"

"We'll find more."

"You'll have to."

"Are you in?" asks Keel. Skipper Williams looks down at his blue cat. She cost him a guinea some ten years ago. His daughter has named her Kathryn because Williams simply calls her Kat. If he goes to sea again, she will come also, like she always did.

He's not the man he once was, not by a long way, but he knows how to command trawlermen, and he knows the ins and outs of a steam trawler, and he knows where to find fish. Williams has tired of his days in the posh house on the Boulevard with his nattering daughter who has pretentions of being upper middle class. She feared him once, but not anymore, and not at all like her mother did before she died. Skipper Williams is a hard taskmaster because so many were cruel to him. He worked up the ladder from trawling ships and box fleets as far back as 1880 – when men actually were men and used cloth sails to get where they were going. He misses the fear in the sailor's eyes and their blind loyalty. For this, Skipper Williams will go with the *Kestrel* and, if he is sunk by a German U-boat, or the icy waves crack the ship in two and he's swallowed up by the cold North Sea, then so be it, that's what he has wanted all these long years. It will be better to die there than asleep on his warm bed in this big house that he does not want.

"Are you in?" repeats Mr Keel.

Skipper Williams nods.

"Aye," he whispers. "I'll sail."

CHAPTER ONE

It's early Saturday morning and the terrace is cold. This is Millhouse Lane in the little village of Cottingham near Hull. George is up early and alone in the stone floored kitchen. Mother has already made a fire and water is boiling in a black pot, she must have gone to the outhouse. George sits leaning forward on one of the dining chairs and tries to clear his chest. It is one of his coughing fits. They sometimes go on for a while. The hacking rattles his body and hurts his chest as he struggles to breathe between each one.

George has not been well for a while. At times, he coughs all night long and his twin brother Sam complains, but not last night. They tipped ale down their necks at the King Billy with the same rag tag bunch that is always there: the Ashwell lads, Jason Williamson, Chiz Isgate and the rest. A rowdy time was had, and old Bullhead himself, the landlord, bought them all a drink. Now they have both turned eighteen, they're old enough to sign up for the Great War, and so what they're about to do deserved a free pint, even if it is the end of the barrel and Bullhead has to use it before next weekend. Sam was too pissed up to complain about his brother's coughing.

George manages to get his chest under control, stands, dips a mug into the warm water for a drink, then sits back down. He's dressed in his Sunday clothes even though it's not Sunday. The coughing fit stopped him putting on his tie. Today he is going to the recruitment office at City Hall. Opposite the statue of Queen Victoria that looks over the square, he is going to sign up to fight in the war.

Sam comes down the stairs dressed in his nightgown with woolly socks on his feet. He looks hungover. Like those who live with each other, they don't exchange any pleasantries. He fills a mug with water and sits down opposite his brother. They both have the same brown hair with grey blue eyes and they're both just under six foot tall. George is thinner than his brother, where Sam got all the strength and charm, he got all the brains. The story is that George's mum delivered them both right here in the kitchen because it was the only warm room in the house, George was first and Sam came out second; that's why he is always late and never seems to know what he's doing. Sam sets down his mug after he's finished the water and gives a big beaming smile from under his crew cut.

"How are you feeling?" he asks his brother.

"Fine," says George. "I wasn't in the state you were." Last night, like always, it was George who picked his brother up from the mud and then they staggered home along Northgate while Sam nattered and blubbered, drunk and wet like some slippery eel from the river. "Do you remember getting back?" he asks. Samuel shakes his head and grins again. He is the little brother in every sense.

Mother walks in through the backdoor. She's small, thin and slightly stooped with a big apron. Her grey hair is done up in a tight bun and there are three eggs in her bony hands from the chickens just in front of the outhouse. Her wrinkled face is without emotion and she sets the eggs down into a bowl by the fire.

"I thought you two would be gone by now," she says.

"The train leaves at half nine," says Sam. It's a five-minute walk down Northgate to the railway tracks from here and then a quarter of an hour into Hull. These two men work at the sawmill like their father did before them, and, when the old man coughed himself to death from tuberculosis two years ago, the foreman offered them both jobs so that their mother would not be put out of the terrace on Millhouse Lane. The three of them are lucky to have this place, and lucky to have jobs at all, and lucky to have each other. Mother is stoney faced as she pokes the fire.

"What'll become of me, with both you two off at war? And only eighteen years old a few weeks ago. I shall lose both of you at once." she doesn't look back at them as she speaks.

They have been through this already.

"You'll have less folk to cook for," says Sam, "and you'll have no more overalls to wash of a weekend." The woman now stares over her shoulder, bird-like, with her eyes beady.

"You've not a thought in your heads for anyone else, neither of you, like your bloody father before." Mother is naturally mean. She is the middle born of seven sisters and can war with words and withering stares, she nags and nips, keeps petty silence when angered, and can argue that night is day if she so wants too.

"We'll not be leaving right away, Mother. Today we'll sign names only and make a promise. There'll be time before we go. You've not to worry." This is George.

"What about Mr Rose, down at the Mill? Why, he promised you lads a job for all your days after your father died. How will he cope when the whole of bloody Cottingham is off with a rifle in their hands." It's not uncommon for Mother to swear but only with the boys.

"For King and Country, Mother," says Sam as he stands up in triumph. He is sunshine bright and warm too with his brown ruffled hair and rich blue-grey eyes. The woman looks up at him and at the corner of her thin mouth is the faintest trace of a smile, because she cannot hide her feelings for him despite how much she tries.

"Youth is wasted on you two," says Mother. "It's a disgrace, it is. You young working men will be off for a jolly in France. You'll be back before summer with a fat belly and a bloody broken liver from all that wine and cheese. You mark my words, Samuel Jackson, you'd better serve this country by looking after your own right here in Cottingham, there's work that needs doing." This is a mid-sized rant from Mother. She can do much better ordinarily, but she will be upset, somewhere behind her stoney frown. Samuel is not like other lads in the village, he wears his heart on his sleeve, like his dad did. He steps forward and puts his arms around his thin

11

mother, then holds her tight as he whispers in her ear:

"I'll be back for you, Mam, I promise."

"You'll need to get dressed before you can go anywhere," she snaps without hugging him back.

At the front door, George stands outside. It's a fine and cold March morning, with a crisp blue sky and the birds from the trees in front nattering at each other. Samuel is already walking away down Millhouse Lane to the station. He will still be a little drunk from the night before. Mother comes to the door behind George and he turns to her. There are no fake words of anger for her first-born lad, she is level with him.

"I'm proud of you this day," she whispers. He nods. Folk round here don't go saying how they really feel. They shouldn't need to – you can see it in their eyes. "But, don't you go telling that bloody fool," she adds as she looks down the lane to Sam who has turned round and is calling to his brother to come.

"I won't," says George.

There's a big queue in Victoria Square. It snakes from the front doors of the great town hall building and around the raised statue of the old queen. In days before, George heard there were speeches, fervent crowds, and soldiers in uniform, all clapping as the men went through the doors and signed up for a war everyone knows is the right thing to do. Inside, he and Samuel will give their details, they'll be examined by a doctor and then take an oath to the King. Sam has explained they'll both be back working at the mill on Monday before training starts proper in a few weeks; men are happier to fight if they can serve with folk from their local area and the battalions are known as pals. In Hull so far, they've raised four of these battalions.

It's not so busy today. The crowds have gone and the volunteers have dwindled from those days last year but there's still support for the war effort. Bullhead at the King Billy told him they'll take men in their mid-fifties and kids who are sixteen as long as they can string a sentence together and stand up. George is not sure how true that is.

The queue feeds in through the huge double doors at the front and then up the main staircase. On the walls are flags and posters with Lord Kitchener's face and his finger pointing out towards the lads. After the war first started back in July last year, the queues were huge with the buzz of anticipation for the fighting and heroics to come. Now there are not so many and perhaps twenty men wait behind George. They are shown to a line of chairs in front of an office and told to sit down. They will wait to be called in by the army doctor for their physical in groups of six. It takes ten minutes. Sam goes through with the first group, and George watches as he disappears behind the frosted glass. George is called through in the next lot.

The doctor is very matter of fact. He has an angular face and a grey moustache. He gets a penny for everyman that he examines whether they go off to fight or not, and he has seen so many now, that the faces and names all blur into one. George lines up with the other men after they have stripped to their pants. He gives his details while the doctor makes notes and then he takes George's height with a stadiometer on wheels. The army doctor smells of cigar smoke and aftershave, his white coat is freshly pressed and his shirt has been starched. The doctor looks up and down his thin body and then uses a cold stethoscope to examine the chest. He coughs on request and the doctor listens to both sides then his back. He taps and hears the phlegm inside the lungs, then looks at George's hands, and at the end of his fingers. If this doctor has discovered something then his face gives nothing away.

In half an hour George waits outside in the late morning watching the other men queue. They're dockers with dirty faces and hands, trawlermen with handkerchiefs around their necks and braces over thick jumpers. There are smartly dressed gents with ties and long jackets, smoking pipes and reading newspapers as they wait. There are kids too, and a man with white hair carrying a walking stick. They all want to fight.

From the double doors of the City Hall, Sam walks past two soldiers on guard towards George with his customary wide grin.

"That doctor's hands were cold," he says. Sam likes to state the obvious that most folk are scared to. "How come you're out before me?" he asks.

"It was quick. I didn't get in," says George. He was not required to take an oath with other men and rejected within the first five minutes. The smile drops from his brother's face and he frowns as if he doesn't understand.

"What do you mean?"

"My chest—there's something up with me. I've been coughing up blood." For the first time in a good long while, Sam Jackson doesn't have anything to say.

They take the train back to Cottingham and in their compartment there's a group of four young men who have been to the recruitment office as well. They sit in a line opposite the two Jackson brothers. They're full of it. George can smell the drink on them even though it's only just after twelve. The two big ones talk in loud voices about what they'll do to the Germans and the Kaiser once they get over there—it's all hot air and shite because they've had a couple of whiskeys. They don't realise that there will be months of training before they get given a uniform and a gun. Sam starts talking to them right away because he'll natter to anyone, that's why folk like him. The biggest lad with the mean eyes and a missing front tooth asks them a question:

"You both signed up, did you?" he says across the carriage. Sam is straight without thinking:

"I'm all in," he says, "but there's something wrong with my

14

George's chest here." Sam nods towards his very slightly older brother. He gives too much away in his words and his facial expressions too, he's a tough lad, but the truth just seems to spill out of him as if he thinks everyone is on his side. The information ignites anger in the mean one. These are young men, not at all fighting lads. They don't know how it is to get belted in the face or bust their knuckles on someone else's jaw; but because there are a few of them together they turn into bullies.

"He's a coward then, is he?" asks one with ginger hair. George cocks his head and responds:

"They wouldn't let me sign up. Not my choice, fella." The biggest one puffs his mouth as if this is bollocks.

"You're shitting it," says the ginger kid. George darkens and takes a deep breath into his thin chest through his nose. There's arrogance to this young man in front, he's rude and sour, as if he's already won the whole war by just signing his name and having a doctor hold his balls while he coughed.

George is not a hot head like his brother Sam, but he's spent time in pubs and among working men who fight and push each other around. He'll have to do something, for his own self-respect if nothing else, and he gathers his right hand into a fist at his side.

"He'll be shitting it," repeats the ginger man. "You're a coward, that's what you are." It's Sam who reacts. His legs power him up and off the train seat as his right fist lashes out to belt the ginger man. Sam hits him square on the nose and the fellow's head snaps back and smacks the wall of the train compartment with a hollow thud. They go at it for a minute or so as the train rattles past the cemetery off Spring Bank West, it's all flailing and motion from Sam's fists. By the time they've got to the Thwaite Street crossing, Sam is standing over the fella looking down on him with his nostrils flared. He's blowing hard and the ginger man's face is a mess.

The Jackson lads don't speak as they walk back from the station to Millhouse Lane. They go down the side of the railway track towards Northgate and past the station master's house on the corner. The silence is loud.

"You should have let me hit him," says George.

"I wish I had. I felt his nose break under my fist."

"Well, thanks."

"You've looked after me enough times, it's only right that I do the same." This is the truth. George plays the role of big brother ordinarily. His younger sibling gets into trouble and he bails him out. "I'm as scared as you are," continues Sam, "but I can't have people talking like that about you." Sam speaks before he thinks. George stops and lets his brother walk on a few paces before the younger lad turns around. "What is it?" he asks.

"You think I'm scared? Am I a coward to you as well?" Sam looks at his brother there in the dull winter sunlight. He has the top button on his shirt done up tight and his brown hair perfectly combed. His face is pale. George doesn't make mistakes; he doesn't get it wrong and he doesn't take chances.

"I don't know," says Sam. It's not meant to sound accusing. He really doesn't know. He can see the worry on his brother's face when he says this.

"I'm not a coward, Sam. The doctor said I wasn't fit to go on account of my coughing."

"Then you're not a coward." Sam has heard his brother wheeze and splutter into his handkerchief many times. He didn't think it was anything serious.

"I'll go back tomorrow," says George. "I'll go back tomorrow and that doctor can look at me again. He can check me over one more time, and he'll see that I'm fine and I'm well. I'll be joining you, Sam. One way or another, we'll be out there together." Sam gives his brother a wide and bright smile.

CHAPTER TWO

Big Billy's mother and father met in Sunday school at St Mary's Church, Etton, in 1891, and they were married the next summer just before Billy was born. They're farm working folk. That's why Billy's dad was so big and couldn't add up properly unless it was money. They sent Billy to Etton school, and he was what the master called 'a daft lad'. He didn't mean this in any sort of endearing way because Big Billy really does struggle with writing and adding; his father couldn't read and neither can his mum, even though she says she can.

The village of Etton is out in the back of beyond, way past Beverley town, and even further out from North Burton over the rolling chalk hills of the Wolds where nothing much happens, ever. Big Billy weathered the school two days a week until he was fifteen and sometimes Sunday school as well. He was a big lad and needed on the farm in the livery yard and out in the fields behind the tractor. At seventeen, he ate more than two people put together and was six foot three but stocky with big arms and floppy blonde hair that fell over his eyes.

Billy's father had been for a good drink out at the Light Dragoon in Etton one Saturday night and, with a flea in his ear about something or other, he clattered his wife around the tiny cottage in the early morning. Billy wouldn't have it, and he was big enough to drag his old man out into the dark morning lane and batter him senseless. It was the first time that Billy really understood how strong he was, and also, that he didn't have to put up with his father's anger and nor did his mother.

The next week, regular as clockwork, the school master scoffed and complained when Billy couldn't read a line from the blackboard. Billy waited till all the other kids had gone, and then, he grabbed the thin school master by his neck and pinned him to the wall while he belted him in the stomach. When the copper from Beverley came out to talk to him and his mam, Billy threatened to clobber him as well.

Now, Billy is not a bad lad, and he would be the first to say that he's not the sharpest tool in the shed, but he isn't a monster like his father. He'll treat people as he's treated by them. That's why his mam in the cottage at Etton gets most of his wage from his livery yard job up at the big house, and why his little sister doesn't have to worry about anything when she walks home from choir practice in the dark—nobody would dare put a hand on her with Billy as her brother. It couldn't carry on this way though. The copper from Beverley, PC James, was a good and proper policeman who knew he could just have a word with Billy to set him straight, and hopefully smooth everything over. It worked for a year or so.

PC James stands outside the little cottage and bangs on the wooden front door with his fist. He doesn't want to be here on a Sunday morning. The door opens and a woman with a shawl across her shoulders, mucky red hair and wonky teeth looks into the early morning at the copper. She knows him. This is the man who always comes for her son, Billy, when he's done something wrong.

"Where is he?"

"Who?" she answers. The crooked teeth affect the way she speaks.

"What do you mean, who? Billy? Where is he?"

"He didn't come home last night," she lies.

"It's serious this time, Judy? I mean it. He's killed a man."

"My Billy? He wouldn't do that."

"He has. Out in Beverley last night. He was fighting again. Talk is that he took on four men outside the White Horse, and he smashed one of them into the cobbles—it shattered his skull. He died this morning at Beverley Hospital, Judy. It'll be murder." The woman looks pale suddenly and her brow creases with worry. If Billy goes to jail, how will she get by?

"I told you, he's not here, are you deaf in the ears?"

"If he is there, Judy, or you've seen him, tell him that this will get worse if he runs. He can plead manslaughter if he comes in now, but if he runs and we have to catch him…" PC James shakes his head, "he could hang." The copper takes a deep breath as he looks up at the woman holding the door open in the little cottage. Maybe he could have done more to help Billy before all this. For a moment he thinks she might open up to him, but she reverts to type:

"I've told you, I haven't seen nor heard of him since yesterday afternoon." PC James looks down the muddy lane and then back to her.

"If you're hiding him, Judy, you'll be an accessory to it all, that means you'll be in trouble as well."

"How many bloody times?" she yells. "He's like his father, he's buggered off."

"Do you want to know who the man was?" PC James wears a frown. This is serious.

"I don't care who he was," she calls as she steps back and slams the door. PC James blinks in the early Sunday morning sunshine and walks back to the car parked some way off down the lane.

Big Billy stands at the top of the stairs in the little cottage looking down on his mother, he takes up all of the space wherever he is in this house. Her face is stone as she looks up.

"As soon as the policeman has driven off, Billy, you've to leave. Give it legs as fast as you can." The big man's straight blonde hair is over his eyes. He's confused.

"I heard him say I should turn myself in."

"Didn't you also hear him say you'd hang?"

"Only if I run," he calls back.

"They'll hang you if they catch you Billy, that's what happens to poor folk like us. You'll have to go."

"Where?"

"I don't bloody know, you should have thought about that when you battered that bloke last night outside the White

Horse. I told you about drinking, Billy, it doesn't mix with this family." She is angry. He is her only boy, and a good one at that when he is not on the ale. He looks confused there at the top of the stairs. He's not prepared for this.

"There were four of them," he says. His mother is suddenly calm:

"They won't give a toss, Billy. You'll go to jail and then you'll hang. If you want to live, you have to give it them two big legs and run." He blinks down on her in the darkness of the stairwell. "Who was it, the man you hit?" Billy looks pale.

"I didn't mean to, it was him who started it, like it always is."

"Who was it, Billy? I'll not ask again. You're a straight lad and I need a straight answer." She has seen Billy look like this before, he knows he has done wrong, but he cannot help himself.

"It was my dad," he whispers. Judy nods and steps up to the big man at the top of the stairs. They embrace. She might lose a son in all this, but at least her husband won't put his hands all over her ever again.

"Where will I go, Mam?" asks Billy as he holds her tight.

"Kingston Upon Hull," she whispers, "get on a boat."

You know where you are on Flinton Street. It's just off Hessle Road and a ten minute walk from St Andrew's Dock. Fishermen and their families live here, but it's no idyllic coastal village where the men wear knitted, roll necked jumpers and white sailor's hats. This is Hull.

The terraced houses are crammed next to each other and squeezed into these little streets where you live right on top of everyone else. Mothers and grandmas wash the front steps and pavement down, kids play hopscotch in the road, and you can always smell the distant whiff of the catch from the docks half a mile away. It's noisy. The rent is cheap. You sleep in a room with your three brothers and the toilet is at the bottom of the garden and shared with the next few houses. Once a week you get washed in a tin bath that hangs on the kitchen wall, if you're lucky, and you share the water with the whole family as well.

Folk are poor, of course, but they're proud of who they are and what their family does. You know everyone and everyone knows you, so that if you ever kissed a girl from Havelock Street behind the sheds at school, your big sister will know by the time you get home. There'll be a thick ear from your mam if you've been too clever to anyone on Hessle Road, and a wallop from your big brother if he's home from sea. You run errands for the old lass who can't make it to the shop. Your mam looks after the kids from next door but three down. There are plenty of folk you're related to, but you don't know how, and so many aunties that you lose track. Your mam lends folk money when the catch has been shite, and she borrows too when your old man hasn't earned enough for you to get by. You know these people. You eat together at Christmas in the front room that's way too small for so many bodies. You go to the weddings up at St Winifred's on Boulevard. There's a street party for the coronation of George V in the June of 1911 and it rains.

You look after each other because nobody else will. When that man from the dock office comes walking down the street with his long cane and black hat, with his collars stiff and starched, and his moustache like a handlebar over his grimacing face, you know that it's awful news, and that if he taps on your door, then it's your dad or uncle or big brother who's been lost at sea.

Tommy knows all this well enough.

It's happened to him.

Tommy doesn't remember the date, but his mam says it was 1905, his father and older brother were aboard the *Golden Era*. It was a steam trawler that left Iceland just before Christmas and should have been home before New Year but the ship was never heard of again. They have Christmas, and New Year passes too, then it is mid-February before the official from the docks comes to visit with his cane and black suit. Things change from then. There are sorry looking faces, and extra hugs from the big aunties who have husbands and sons away at sea as well. There is a bag of sweets for Tommy and his two sisters.

Without the main breadwinners of his father and elder brother, the Woods family can no longer afford the rent, and even if they had the money, they can't stay without a man in the house. There is little Tommy, his mam and the two older girls at seven and thirteen. Because the Hessle Road community is the way it is, nobody will see them go without, so someone takes them in.

They move to Tyne Street, to the biggest end terrace at the bottom, with Cousin Mathews, a big ex-trawlerman in his sixties with a fat gut and a small, shy wife. It is charity of course—Mathews doesn't have the space for another four bodies in a three bedroomed house with four in already. Tommy's mam takes work in the patty factory and so does his eldest sister when she is fourteen a year later. The family shares the box room and sleeps head to foot.

Tommy has to get used to a man who is nothing like his father, for Mathews is loud and rude to the six women who live in his house. He bleats like some swollen, pasty lord with his fat gut, flabby face, and thin white beard. If Tommy goes anywhere near him, he lets out a clip with one of his big fisherman's hands that have worked the trawl winch and fixed nets in the freezing cold arctic for more than forty years. Mathews is entitled too, because this is his house that he pays for, and the food on the table is given by his grace and charity to a poor, ratty little lad like Tommy. If there's nobody to see, and he's not quick enough, old cousin Mathew's will grab Tommy Woods by his skinny wrists and slap him round the head and face till he cries, the old man says it's character

22

building. Unlike Tommy's dad who showed up every three months or so with a big, solid grin, Mathews never leaves the house on account of his arthritis.

In the box room of the end terrace and listening to Mathews shout at his little wife in the night, Tommy brings his knees up to his chest and waits for the day he'll go to sea like his dad. Then, with his first wage, he'll come back down Tyne Street and rescue his mam and his sisters. They'll go back to Flinton and Tommy will be like his dad, a warm and big lad with a wide smile, and eyes that twinkle in the sunshine.

Tommy is unlucky.

At fourteen you can get work as a bobber on the docks. These are the lads and men who land the fish from the trawlers when they come in. It's a steady job. Unlike fishermen, you get to go home every night and don't risk your life on the open seas so, positions like this are in demand. Belowmen go down into the fishrooms and pack and sort the fish into baskets, on the dock is a winchman who controls the crane to bring it up out of the hold. There's a swinger who pushes the baskets across to the tipper who catches it and pours it into a ten stone kit bucket then weighs it. They're unionized lads and so the pay is good, but they're tough with it and the humour is cruel. They wear clogs to stop their feet slipping and start work at two in the morning because you want to keep the fish as cold as you can and get it ready for the fish market at seven thirty.

It's a way for Tommy to earn money before he goes off to sea himself, bobbers and trawlermen don't always see eye to eye, but they know this Woods boy and they know that he lost his brother and his dad on the same boat years before. Tommy turns up at half one in the morning for a week hoping that they need someone extra. He keeps his head down when the other bobbers take the piss as they do, because if he waits there long enough, they will have to give him a job. With his first week's wage, Tommy is going to buy the biggest piece of beef steak he can and hope that Mathews will choke on it.

It happens the Wednesday, the first day they give him a job as a barrow lad. All he has to do is load the baskets they call kits onto a hand cart and take them down to the fish markets some hundred yards away. Tommy wants to impress. He is a trier. He struggles with the handcart because he's not quite strong enough to push it, so the foreman gets him on board the trawler. He's going to get the lad to go down into the fishroom and fill the buckets for them to winch up. Tommy is keen, but as green as they come, so the poor sod loses his footing at the top of the hatch and falls right down into the fishroom when it's nearly empty. It's a ten-foot drop at least. The foreman has to go down and get him. Tommy Woods has cracked his ankle badly and his face is red from trying not to cry, he can't walk on it properly, so the foreman has to send him home.

The bobbers watch him limp away from the dock and shake their heads—his first day, he's an unlucky bastard is Tommy Woods.

He still can't put any weight on it after a week, or after two. In a month, Tommy's mam takes him to the doctor in town, and she pays the two-guinea fee out of her savings. The fat doctor pokes around at the ankle and the twisted blackened foot and sucks in air as he shakes his head in dismay. It's a break. They should have come sooner. It'll have to come off or young Tommy will lose a leg, and most probably die.

The Woods are good folks aye, but it doesn't just rain on them, it's a full on storm. After he's lost his foot, Tommy uses a stick everywhere he goes and by seventeen, he's the spitting image of his old man, only he walks with a limp on a fake wooden prosthetic that he was gifted from the hospital on Anlaby Road. He's worked the trawlers already, six trips altogether and he knows his way around a ship, but skippers are wary because folk say bad luck follows him like a cloud. The disability means he's slower than other men as well, so Tommy only gets a job if he's absolutely the last fisherman on the dock side, they'd rather take an old sea dog or a young kid than Tommy. He thought by now he'd be able to make some real money.

At seventeen, Mathews expects Tommy to pay rent for his mother and his older sister. The eldest has married already and moved away to be with her new husband leaving just the three of them in that little box room. Tommy can see the disappointment in his mam's eyes when he is not away at sea, and the arrogance of Mathews hangs in the house like the stink of his swollen liver from all the mild he drinks. It's no life living there. He watches his mother shrivel up as she works in the patty factory, and his sister is sullen with her rotten front teeth that they can't afford to fix. Then, there's Tommy, who fell into a fishroom when he was fourteen, his first day on the job as well.

Now the war has broken out, Mathews goes on and on about how he would sign up to fight if he was young enough, and how Tommy is a right disappointment because his limp stops him from going. He says Tommy's dad would look down on him from heaven with a heavy broken heart at the sight of his son who can't properly walk or get regular work.

In March 1915, Mathews hears from neighbours that a steamer called the *Kestrel* is sailing in a week or so for a trip to Ireland. He suggests Tommy, not because he thinks he's a good trawlerman but so that the lad can earn money to pay him rent, or better still, he can be swept overboard in a swell and never come home. Tommy will take the job, of course, he has to.

His mother finds him in the backyard the Saturday before he's due to sail. He's packing his kitbag with his waterproofs and extra socks, he remembered that his mother used to do this for his older brother and his father, but things have changed, Tommy does this for himself. His mother comes up behind him. She's short with mousey brown hair, and over these last few years she has tried to make herself invisible.

"It's good you've got a trip," she says. Tommy Woods kneels down as he rolls one of his sweaters up tight to fit into his kit bag. "You've to be careful," she says.

"I will be." His mother stands behind him with her hands together. She is nervous. She has something to tell him but she does not know quite how to get started. He stands to face her. "You've to make some money on this trip, Tommy," she says. "Mathews says he's sick of you being here, he says you're a man now and you should be looking after your own."

Tommy nods. He's heard this already.

"Is that what you think?"

"It doesn't matter what I think, Tommy. This is his house and where else have I got to go? You can't come back with a bad catch or with nowt, or else…" she swallows before she says this, "it'd be better if you didn't come back at all." Tommy winces. "I've done my best for you all, Tommy, I really have, but Mathews won't keep us any longer." He looks down on the mousey haired woman who has defended him all these years.

"I'll get us out of this, Mother," he says. "You'll see. I'll come home with enough money to set us up somewhere new."

"You'll bloody have to, Tommy," she says.

CHAPTER THREE

It's just after six in the morning, the day before she'll sail and Peter Everett is down in the engine room of the *Kestrel* giving it the once over. This is his first time on the trawler, but he knows his steam engines alright and this one has definitely seen better days. With his shaky hands, he checks the pipes and the boiler, the triple cylinders and the prop shaft that spins the propellor outside in the cold water. He gives her a bit of a clean down as well and his glasses slip off his nose due to his constant shaking. He's learned to get used to it over the last few months. Tonnes of coal have already been dumped into the coal room, that's why the *Kestrel* is so low in the water already. He's been told the first mate, John Grace, will be there as well.

After twenty minutes, he hears footsteps on the deck above and the hatch to the engine room opens. Peter Everett walks round the cold boiler to the ladder leading up from the darkness.

"How's it looking down there?" calls a voice from above.

"It's been cold for weeks," he yells up. Peter Everett climbs the iron ladder to the person standing above with shaky hands and legs. He clambers up on deck and stands in front of the figure; the late winter sky is grey and moody above.

"You'll have to get her fired up straight away."

"You must be the first mate."

"I am, name's John Grace." They don't shake hands. He's a Scouser in his sixties with grey, balding hair and colourless pale skin. He has a bit of a gut and a limp. His accent isn't the hard Liverpudlian rasp but something softer even though it's clear where he's from. In the past people took the piss out of his girl's second name, and this helped make him strong and focused. "We're to sail Monday, she has to be ready by then." Peter Everett nods. He's good with engines and machines, he has a delicate and clever touch that they seem to listen to. His head judders as if he is shivering. He's not cold. Grace regards the engineer.

"I'm Peter Everett."

"What's wrong with you?" he asks. Peter Everett is in his late forties, he's tall and slender so he has to bend down to go through the engine room door below. He wears round glasses and has an intelligent face. He shakes all the time, just a wobble, but a definite shudder. His head moves up and down continuously and his hand judders at his side. Grace is not sure how much he wants to sail with such a man.

"What's wrong with me?" repeats Peter Everett. He doesn't answer the question right away. The absolute truth is that he does not know. In September 1914, six months earlier, Peter Everett was an engineer aboard the *HMS Pathfinder* in the North Sea. They were hit by a torpedo. He was below deck when it happened and the vessel went down like a stone, him with it. He can't really remember. At first the fishermen who rescued him thought he was shivering because of the cold, but he didn't stop, and hasn't stopped shaking since. Peter Everett is embarrassed by himself like any middle-class Englishman is, and more so that he was discharged from the navy on medical grounds. He's a long way from being a coward.

"I've got the shakes," he says.

"I can see that," says Grace. Peter Everett could explain what happened to him to mitigate the fact that he shakes like he does, but the Scouse first mate will not understand, like Peter's wife doesn't understand.

"I'm fit to sail and I know my engines," he says. John Grace half snarls as he inspects Peter Everett. "I'm here to do a job."

"Have you been drinking?"

"No." The Scouser stands closer to him:

"Everyone likes a few," says Grace, "but if I catch you boozing on duty, I'll put you overboard." His words are barbed and sharp.

It's the pan calling the kettle. John Grace is sixty-four, he shouldn't be going to sea because his body isn't up to it. His knees are shafted, that's why he has a limp. They won't let him enlist and, of course he wants to help the war effort, so the next best thing he can do is fish, like he always has. There is something else, it's a gambling debt from card games he's had over at the Dairycoates Inn off Hessle Road. Grace is here to earn and then sort the debt. The landlady at the pub says that if he can't pay, someone will take a hammer to his hands, then if he can't pay again, it will be his feet, and finally, his face. Grace is a straight man. He wants it sorted, quickly. He's been a skipper himself out of Fleetwood, and a first mate out of Grimsby, he worked on the box trawlers and sailed the cutters that took the fresh fish down the Thames. He knows his ships and he knows his fishing. There's no time for jokes or idle chat with John Grace. He just wants to catch the fish, land it and get paid.

Peter Everett looks down on the serious first mate through his round glasses.

"I don't drink," he says. "I just shake. That's why I'm here. The navy doesn't need me anymore."

"You mean they don't want you? Which ship?" asks Grace.

"*HMS Pathfinder*."

"How come you aren't there?"

"She took a torpedo."

"Were you onboard?"

"Yes," says Peter Everett. The two regard each other for a moment. "What's your excuse?"

"I'm sixty-four." Both of these sailors know that the *Kestrel* will sail with the only available crew that the ship's husband can find, and that they will be old men or boys, or worse. John Grace is already aware who the skipper will be. He's worked with Williams in the past, and he knows that the stories about him are true, but at his age, Grace is unsure of how the old man will cope. He looks back to Peter Everett who shakes as he stands on deck:

"Can you do the job, son? I mean if you can't then we can find someone else, but for the sake of the other men who'll sail on this ship, you have to be up to it." Peter Everett would have struggled to answer this question before he was torpedoed and nearly drowned, now he has to tell the truth.

"I can work a steam engine better than most. I know how they go and whistle and buzz. Mr Keel knows that I shake, but you don't get to be second engineer on a scout cruiser like the *Pathfinder* without knowing a thing or two, Mr Grace. How many ships have you worked on that had a complement of over two hundred and fifty men?" Peter Everett delivers this little speech with his shaking head and blinking eyes. He has defended himself.

"Nothing more than twenty hands," says John Grace, "but none of them sank." He can be cruel. He doesn't quite know what happened on the *Pathfinder*, and anyway, he's stamping his authority on this tall man who is meant to be the engineer. John Grace is the first mate and second in command. When the skipper isn't on the bridge, this will be his ship.

"How about you just do your job and I'll do mine?" says Peter Everett. He was a quiet and retiring man even before the shaking affliction and the torpedo incident but he has confidence in his experience, he's been a naval engineer for the best part of twenty-five years. John Grace nods his head:

"Just as long as you can do your job," he adds. Peter Everett tries to keep his head level but it's shaking left to right and up and down. He expected trouble from the fishermen but he didn't expect it so soon. If he could, Peter Everett would walk off the *Kestrel* and catch the train back to Bridlington by the sea, but he's not welcome there in his present state, his wife has made that much clear.

"I'll have this engine cleaned and fired up by this afternoon, she'll be all ready to go tomorrow morning. If you're not happy with that, I'll be on my way. You just let me know." John Grace likes this answer.

"I will," he says.

A fat man approaches from the port side of the ship. His black hair is a little long at the back and he hasn't shaved for a few days. He's wearing a tatty brown overcoat and carries a duffle bag over his shoulder as he waddles down the gangplank and steps on board. He gives both men a grin as he walks past, and one of his front teeth is blue and black rotten. There's the whiff of sweat and fags on him as he goes past.

"That's Stout," says John Grace, "the cook." Peter Everett attempts a wince but his shaking means it doesn't quite come off and it looks like a smile. They watch the cook lumber to the steps into the galley and mess room, and then look back at each other with a sense of unease. They hear him stomp down below deck and into the kitchen, he begins whistling and the sound is tuneless in the early morning.

"What's the rest of the crew like?" asks Peter Everett.

"The same kind of thing," says John Grace. Anyone else might crack a smile at this, but until the money is in his hand, the Scouse first mate is not going to give an inch of himself. Peter Everett nods. It's like that then. He turns and shakes his way down the ladder to the engine room.

It's mid-afternoon and Peter Everett has spent the best part of the morning working on the engine. The boiler of the *Kestrel* has been cold for a few weeks, perhaps more. It's not been looked after, there's too much grease on the prop shaft and the cylinders are filthy. Peter Everett likes the noise of an engine room and this one is silent. It's unnerving somehow.

At half past two, he hears someone open the hatch and come down the ladder to the boiler. There's a scraping sound coming from the coal room—steam trawlers like the *Kestrel* need tonnes of the stuff to get them out into the far seas and they also need someone to shovel it into the furnace. Peter Everett walks into the dark coal room and there's a short figure with a shovel standing beside the door. He wears a filthy paperboy style black cap that covers his eyes and a donkey jacket.

"Can I help?" says Peter Everett. This is his middle-class way of saying 'who are you?'.

"Cooper. Trimmer and fireman," says the figure. The voice sounds young. He holds out a hand and Peter Everett shakes it. He's friendly at least. In the weak light from the hatch above, he can see the little man is already blackened and Cooper's paperboy cap is just above his eyes. The trimmer keeps all the coal level on a boat so it doesn't tip over in the water, and the fireman shovels it into the furnace. It's not just a hard job, you have to know how a boat rests in the water and it's more than just shovelling the coal into the fire as well, you need to work the flames depending on where the air flow is. Cooper is just under five foot, it's the perfect size for clambering about in the coal room.

"I've trimmed her already, I was here yesterday," says Cooper. "I've raked the furnace out too. She's ready for lighting."

"I'm Peter Everett, the engineer," he says by way of introduction.

"I know. You've got the shakes because you got hit by a torpedo. *HMS Pathfinder*, was it?" There are no secrets on a ship like the *Kestrel*. John Grace would have told him already. "Two hundred and sixty one deaths," says Cooper as if Peter Everett wouldn't know.

"Something like that," he answers. He does not want to talk about it. He would rather not remember it either.

"I've heard you know your engines."

"That, I do. Have you worked the *Kestrel* before?"

"This is my ship," answers Cooper. "I worked up from being a deck hand six years ago. I know her just as if she was my own mam. She looks a sight but she can sail."

"Who was the engineer last? He left it in a right state. I've been at the prop shaft and the cylinders for an hour."

"He was a chancer at best, a fella named Bacon, had some German in him too and his father ran the butcher's shop on Princess Ave. He proper ran when the war started." Peter Everett shakes as he listens. Anyone with any link to Germany will get their head kicked in, given half a chance. That butcher's shop has had its windows put through more than a few times.

"I've nearly got her ready, but I'll need a bit more time to check the movement, better I do it now than before she's hot." Peter Everett will have to make sure that everything works as it should, for when the pistons begin to drive the prop shaft and the propeller, he will not be able to. It's tiny compared to the *HMS Pathfinder*, it won't take him long.

Cooper cocks his head as he examines Peter Everett who is standing, shaking as he does with his head moving up and down and side to side. Cooper smiles and Peter Everett can see the blackened teeth in the darkness, he isn't taking the piss, it's friendly. Here is someone who may be even stranger than Cooper himself is.

"I'll give you a hand. Have you got a nickname?"

"I'm Peter." Cooper nods. It's not good to call people by their real names on a trawler, it's unlucky.

"What about you?"

"I'm Cooper."

"Is that your nickname?"

"If you like."

CHAPTER FOUR

Big Billy fought his father before, on many occasions. The man was a heavy hitter if he could get one on you, and if he'd been drinking, he didn't feel pain. Billy caught him an uppercut on the chin that Saturday night, it snapped his head back so the flat cap fell off. The old man went as stiff as a board, with his hands out, and he cracked his skull on the cobbles as he hit them. Billy didn't know he was dead. He was sure he'd have to fight the old man again one day. Now he won't have to, not ever.

Billy cut across the fields this morning. He made it to the train station between North Burton and Etton and hopped on the back of the empty goods steam engine from York that was heading to Beverley. Billy hid under a sack on one of the open wagons and it was cold but didn't rain at least. That's where he is now.

He peeps out from under the sack every time they stop and notes the names of the stations if he gets the chance, Billy's not that sure he can read them properly. The signs are Beverley then Cottingham then Hull, where the train stops. Billy thinks about throwing off the sack and legging it, but there are too many people, then it starts moving again.

It's freezing cold as the train rattles along the track but Billy has killed a man, and for that, the coppers will search for him until he's found and then he'll be hanged. In the late afternoon when it's already dark, the train stops dead and he hears the noise of railroad carriage doors opening far down the other end along with men's voices.

This is where he gets off, and in the light of the fading afternoon, he stumbles away to hide behind a stack of crates. Billy looks at the sign on the station in the dim light and makes out the words 'St Andrew's Dock'. The steam engine was dragging empty carriages, now it's time to fill them up, and Billy can hear gangs of lads working and moving closer. His legs tingle from lying down so long, and his hands are cold. Hunger gnaws at his stomach.

Billy sees the lights from the huge fishing boats moored up on the quayside of St Andrew's Dock and smells the fresh fish. He doesn't know where he is and he's a mixture of afraid and tired at the same time. He moves away from the railway tracks and towards the lights of a much bigger building in the distance. He can hear voices on the wind around him and the hiss of other engines moving off.

Unlike where Billy comes from, St Andrew's Dock is alive with life at this time of the day, like it is most of the time. After climbing over a six-foot wooden fence, he finds the road and walks towards a gas streetlight mounted over a door on a huge building with a corrugated iron roof. As he gets closer, he sees there are men going in and out. There's the smell of cooking too and the noise of chatting and people eating. He follows the smell, and before he knows it, he's standing outside, in front of a pale looking man in fish worker's overalls who's smoking a cigarette. Billy doesn't quite know what to say.

"What do you want?" asks the fella as he sees Billy looking at him. If this were a pub, he'd say something a bit nasty back, but here, where he is on unfamiliar ground, and after he's murdered his own dad, he doesn't say anything at all. "Are you looking for the office?" asks the fella. "I mean are you looking for a job?" This seems like a good idea.

"Aye," says Billy. The man is instantly more friendly. "Go round the side of the building here and there's the office. Tell them you want a job and they'll sort you out." Billy nods.

It doesn't take long at all for him to walk to the office of the Humber Steam Trawling Company. It's not uncommon for men to turn up for work at this time given that they often set sail early in the morning. They might have come in on another ship or by train, and there's a place for them to doss down as well.

He says his name is Billy Thorne, and the man in the office

with his glasses on the end of his nose writes it down as William. He gives a fake date of birth too and says he comes from Beverley. They need workers, but not to be bobbers on the docks or the men who load the steam engine carriages—these are unionized lads and it's not easy to get into these jobs; they need trawlermen, and no experience is required because they'll teach you while you're out there. Not everyone wants to do this because going out into the North Sea is dangerous, especially in winter, and especially when there is a war on. The office man explains that lots of fishing trawlers have been requisitioned by the Admiralty along with their crews. When he sees that Billy doesn't get what he's on about, he tells him they need fishermen because lots have gone off to train or fight in the war. Both of these are true.

He tells Billy that he'll spend the night in the Royal Mission and get a hot meal, breakfast as well. Then, Monday morning, he'll be off. They'll take all the expenses out the wages he's yet to earn and this seems okay to Billy. Before he knows what's happening, he's been shown to the mission and has had a thin vegetable broth followed by some tough beef and potatoes. Then, he lies on the bottom of a bunk bed in a deserted dorm room, looking up at the springs on the mattress above him.

You couldn't have planned it better. They tell him that tomorrow he'll be off to sea and the ship is called the *Kestrel*. Billy closes his eyes.

With a warm bed, a full belly, and tired legs; he doesn't worry about the future at all.

"What did the doctor say was wrong with you?" asks Mother. George adds more coal to the fire and then sits back down in the wooden chair at the kitchen table. Opposite is Sam eating one of the scones his mother made that afternoon while they were at the recruitment office.

"He didn't say what was wrong with me."

"Well, there must be a reason or he would have signed you

up for the front like everyone else."

"I know that, Mother." Her eyes are hard blue jewels in her thin head. It matters what people think to her and she has to get the story straight for what she will tell the neighbours.

"Did he say anything at all?"

"He said I ought to get myself looked at."

"What for?"

"I don't know, he didn't say."

"Well, that's no good, is it? What kind of doctor doesn't tell you what's wrong with you?"

"Maybe he doesn't know, and it's not his job to say what's wrong with me, he's just there to check that lads are fit to go to war." George is angry. He is angry that he is not well enough to sign up for the front, he is angry with the fight Sam had on the train, and now he is angry with his mother for asking so many questions. He knows she's a hard lass, but there's a sense, like there was with the lads on the train, that George is some sort of coward, and it's he who doesn't want to go off and fight.

"What will I tell the neighbours?"

"Tell them what you bloody like."

"You'll not swear in my house, George Jackson."

"You'll stop bothering me then."

"I'm worried about you, lad. If you're not fit to go to war then there'll be a reason. You'll fetch yourself down to see Dr Micheal on New Street in the morning and let him look at you." George frowns at his mother. Sam takes a slurp on his mug of tea to wash down the scone. He picks up another piece from the plate and puts it in his mouth. "There's nothing wrong with our Sam," says his mother.

"There's never anything wrong with our Sam," says George.

"What's got into you? You're acting like your father would have. We've to get to the bottom of this lad, if you're not fit to go to war then what else are you not fit to do?"

"He said I had a cough."

"A cough?"

"That's what I said."

"There's nothing wrong with a cough, is there? I mean Mr Harris next door coughs all day and night long and he's still fine to go off to work, even at his age."

"Well, that's just what he said."

"You're a young lad. What can be wrong with you? Your brother's fine and fit to go, but you say the doctor wouldn't allow it. What am I to say to the folk in the street? I heard that young Brown lad was there last week, you know, that young Steven Brown from Northmoor Lane, he's not but five foot in big boots and as thin as a rake too, why, they let him in. He's fit to go off to do his duty, but my George, a strapping lad and as fit as a fiddle bow, he's not allowed to because he's got a cough. Do you see how it sounds, George?"

"How does it sound? You tell me mother. It wasn't but five minutes ago that you were teary eyed here in this very room. There you were, crowing that your only two lads were off to war in Fance and would leave you all alone to die, now you've changed your tune. Do you want us to go or not?"

"I want you to do what's right, George. I want it for the people of this town and the people of this country. You young lads have got to go and get this done, by God if I could do it, I sure as hell would."

"The doctor said I couldn't go, mother, have you got cloth in your ears? What part of that do you not understand?"

"He'll have got it wrong, George. Anyone can see there's nothing the matter with you, especially when that Brown lad can get in and you can't." Mother has that way of going and going at a subject until everything is wrought from it and until she gets to the bones of the problem. It made her husband boil like a kettle. It makes George feel like that too.

"Are you saying that I'm lying mother?" This is the heart of it. George does not want to say this, but his mother has

38

forced his hand. He does not like to admit that she thinks so little of him.

"I know what you're like, George," says his mother. This means she thinks he's lying. The young man stands up in anger and the wooden chair scrapes along the stone floor.

"Do you think I'm afraid to go, Mother, is that it?" George has raised his voice.

"It's my fault, George. It was wrong of me to act like I did before and to say what I said." Her voice is also louder, and there's emotion on it like they have not heard in all these years. The old woman is speaking from her heart. "I'll be fine here without you, George. I know you're a good lad and you don't want to leave me all alone here to fend for myself, but I'll be fine. People look after each other in Cottingham, that's the kind of folk we are." Mother comes around the table to stand in front of her son, her eyes look up at him in the little kitchen. She can see the tears forming in his eyes. "You'll have to go, George. You'll have to, whatever happens to me. Tomorrow you'll go down to that office and you'll have that doctor look at you again, and you'll sign up like you should have done today." George swallows. She has misjudged him in every way. She believes he's too weak to leave her, and that he is a liar as well. It's like being spat on. George's face has lost all its colour as he looks down on his mother.

George slams the front door of the house as he leaves so the floorboards above the kitchen rattle. Sam has not got up from his chair and he watches his mother hold her face in her hand just for a fleeting moment as the emotion comes out of her. Women who aren't as hard as she may have shed a tear, but not Mother, she sucks all the pain back up into her stomach and stands up straight. If George does not go, then who will look after Sam, the poor sod can just but tie his shoelaces.

"He'll be back," she announces into the kitchen around her. "Just like his father, he'll see sense and he'll be back."

Mother is not sure. George is much more like she is, and she knows that when he's made up his mind, he won't be swayed from it.

George catches the last train to Hull and the carriages are mostly empty. The big wheels on the track below clatter out into the early evening and the whistle sounds as the train powers back towards Paragon Station. He is doing what he should have done a long time ago—he is leaving. He stayed for the sake of his thin mother and because Sam needed him, now there is no requirement for him to be there at all with his brother going off to war. In the winter of 1912, Mr Elsden from a few doors needed money for his daughter's wedding, so he went down to the mission building just off the docks and signed up for a stint on a deep-sea trawler. He was away for six weeks and came back half-cut with a wallet full of notes and stories of the sea that Mother didn't believe.

That's where George is going.

In the morning at the Royal Mission, Big Billy washes his face in one of the porcelain basins in the huge bathroom. He's wearing braces over a white vest and wide working lad's trousers. Billy had a grand night's sleep without disturbance and he goes back to the bottom bed of the bunk to put on his shirt.

There are only a few other lads here in the big dorm and he follows them down the stairs, and out through a courtyard then into a mess hall where it's just starting to get busy. Men behind a long serving hatch are handing out breakfast, and Billy copies the other workers and goes to stand in the line. A brown-haired man in front turns to him as he joins the queue.

"What you in for?" he asks. The man looks thin and pale but has honest, blue-grey eyes.

"Trawlers," answers Billy.

"Me too," says the lad. He looks a little scared.

"Do you know which one?"

"The *Kestrel*. I came in last night." Billy smiles. He holds out his big hand for the lad to shake.

"Me as well," he says. "My name's Billy."

"I'm George Jackson," says the man with brown hair, "from Cottingham." He hands one of the trays back to Billy and collects one himself.

"You been on a trawler before?" asks Billy.

"I haven't. And you?"

"I've never even been on a boat." He grins. Until you wind Big Billy up, he is a lovely fella.

"Where you from?" here Billy has to remember to lie.

"Beverley," he says.

They sit down opposite each other in the dinner hall with their trays of breakfast, other men know each other, and as the place fills up there's the sound of easy chatter and the clink of knives on tin plates. These are the workers who unload coal and load up fish. It's a big operation.

Billy and George fall into the easy talk of men who are both a little nervous about where they are. George explains that he came from Cottingham last night, he says he needs time away, and to make some money too. Billy doesn't pry and he tells him he lost his job at the livery yard because he belted the farmer's posh knob son. This is true but actually happened last year and he got his job back after a month. Billy's not an expert at lying so he sticks to a version of the truth, that way he won't forget what he's said.

At half seven the gruff foreman finds the two lads chatting over mugs of tea. He tells them the *Kestrel* is ready and they follow him through to the stores where each one collects a long kit bag to carry over their shoulder, these will be full of the waterproofs they'll need for the trip.

"I'm six foot three," says Billy to the store man. "Will they fit?" The man with a straight face and a black moustache just shrugs his shoulders like he couldn't care less.

CHAPTER FIVE

The *Kestrel* sits low in the water at the far side of St Andrew's Dock. She's roped up to one of the fat metal cleats and there are billows of black smoke emptying from her funnel even though she's not moving. Under the deck, Cooper will have lit the furnace and it will be warming up the boiler to start generating steam to drive the engine. Big Billy and George follow another man along the dockside who explains he's the ship's husband, Mr Keel. The dock isn't so busy, to the right they can hear the shouts and calls of winchmen on board a trawler as they swing baskets of fish across to the bobbers. George reads the letters painted on the side, *H87 Gemini*, he wonders how they get their names. Mr Keel barks information over his shoulder as he walks:

"You'll get paid once you get back and your wages will depend on the catch. We'll deduct the cost of the kit you're carrying, along with food and any incidentals that arise as well." George nods, Big Billy doesn't really understand what he's talking about.

As they get closer to the *Kestrel*, they can already see that it's a much smaller boat than the one they just passed. It's about a hundred feet long with rust around the sides just above the water level. The funnel that gently puffs black smoke looks mucky and well-used. At the gangplank, Mr Keel points for them to step on board and go down onto the boat, then he follows.

The *Kestrel* doesn't fill either George or Billy with a great deal of confidence. The deck planks creak and the trawl winch looks black with age and use, there's the smell of stale fish, salt and smoke. The little crew are gathered on the deck in front of the wheelhouse and Mr Keel goes to an old man dressed in an off-white roll neck jumper, he has a flat black cap, a thin face, and a white moustache. Despite his age there's gravity to him so he nods with some petulance when the ship's husband whispers in his ear. Mr Keel steps away from him.

"Gather round," calls this old man. His thin voice is lost in the cold wind but the crew assembled on the deck turn their heads towards him. This must be the skipper. He eyes the two new men who have stepped aboard but does not offer any warmth or greeting. He has a cold stare and his skin is stretched tight across his thin cheeks.

"My name is Skipper Williams," he croaks. He looks like he needs a good hot dinner and a sit down already. "I run a tight ship, by that I mean I don't tolerate dickheads. Do as you're asked and keep your head down. We're to go up over the top of Scotland and down into the Irish Sea, it's a long way but the country needs the fish, and there'll be a pretty penny for you lot in it as well." Skipper Williams has more fire in him than you'd think. George and Billy stand with their long kit bags hooked over their shoulders by the handles. "This man next to me is John Grace, first mate, he'll carry on from here." Grace has got a bit of a gut, glasses and is in his sixties easily but there's a stern, no nonsense way to him. His voice is significantly louder when he speaks:

"I don't deal with dickheads either," he begins. He steps forward to Big Billy and looks him up and down.

"What's your name, son?" Ordinarily, Billy does not do well with authority in any form but, he did murder his father a few days past and he needs to get out of Hull as quickly as he can. He'll be nice:

"Billy Thorne, Sir," he answers. When people first meet Billy, they usually comment on the size of him with something like 'what did your mother feed you?' or 'what bloody size shoe do you take?' There is none of this with Grace. He is here to sail a boat to catch fish, not exchange cheap comments to amuse himself or anyone else.

"And you?"

"George Jackson."

"Either of you two worked a trawler before?" The two men

43

shake their heads. "It's hard graft, but you'll pick it up. Skipper Williams is in charge and I'm his first mate. That tall man shaking like he's wet to the bone is Peter Everett, engineer. The one with the peg foot who doesn't climb ladders properly is Tommy Woods, he's the bosun, that means he looks after all the nets and the stuff on the deck—he moves like shite but knows his boats and he knows more than you. The thirteen-year-old lad there with the rabbit teeth is the fish room man and third hand, his name's Young Jack—he's more senior than either of yous two, so you do what he tells you. The mucky thing in the black cap and big wellies is Cooper, the trimmer. He keeps the coal level so the boat doesn't tip up and he feeds the engine to keep us moving as well—that's why he's filthy. There's a cook too, he's down in the galley, a fat bastard. I'd avoid him if I were you."

George blinks across at this earnest Scouser, he has explained the job on board a trawler in layman's terms, by no means are the duties these men perform simple or easy. "You two are deck hands, you do whatever any of these men ask you to do. Do you understand?" Big Billy winces inside but nods. George is not sure what he thinks, yet:

"Aye," he says.

"We're a friendly lot," adds John Grace. George casts his eyes over the crew, there's the shaking engineer with his head wobbling to and fro, the lame man leaning on the bulkhead of the wheelhouse, a thirteen-year-old lad who could be younger, and a five-foot figure who looks like he has never washed either himself or his clothes. He watches the frail figure of Skipper Williams making his way up the ladder to the wheelhouse where he'll steer the ship. With the grey sky above, these men don't seem friendly at all. Grace sees the sour expression on George's face.

"I know we look like we've just got out of prison," he says, "but this is trawling. We make a lot of money and the work is dangerous and hard. You could have stayed at home with your mam if you'd wanted a nice smile." This is the cruel humour that allows this boat to function, it oils their interactions. Big Billy knows it well. Even before they have set off, the boat seems to rock under George's feet. "Jack here will show you to a bunk," says Grace, and they follow the young lad with buck teeth down the side of the ship.

The waves of the Humber were fairly bad, but now they are out on the sea proper and round Spurn Point, the ship pitches and rises over the green waters of the ocean. George finds himself at the stern of the *Kestrel* looking out at the grey sky and the frothy, deep dark water below. Clutching the rails he dry heaves into the ocean with a retching sound, his eyes water as he does. At least here at the stern he is out of the wind, and away from the stink of the bunk rooms and galley below. George thinks about his mother in the kitchen in the terraced house in Cottingham with her mean eyes and her opinion that he is a coward. He wishes that he'd never come but remembers why he left in the first place. Between the waves and the movement of his stomach, he considers his brother too, who will be going off to train and then fight. How will Sam be this day, without his elder brother there to stop him doing anything stupid? He'll probably cut his thumb off at the sawmill or get into a fight in the pub tonight.

A figure appears out of the corner of his eye moving up the ship. It's the man with the limp, Woods.

"The sickness will pass, mate," he says as he approaches. "I promise."

"How do you know?"

"I was the same on the first trip. Your stomach needs time to catch up with your head." Woods is well meaning and in his late teens with a thin gaunt look—much the same as George. "Where you from?" he asks.

"Cottingham." George wipes his eyes with the sleeve of his coat and looks down at his boots on the slippery deck of the

Kestrel. He wishes he hadn't come, again. The ship crests and falls once more and George grips the railing as his stomach churns like it was making butter. "How many times have you sailed?" he asks.

"Plenty," says Woods. "It's in my family. Not as much as I would have liked owing to this foot." He nods down to his right shoe that looks too big to be real.

"What happened?"

"An accident when I was a lad. It stopped me going to sea proper for a while."

"Kept you away from volunteering for the war as well, I should imagine."

"It did." Woods looks out at the sea behind him when he says this. Expectation crushes these young men when their country thinks they should be away at war, and they're held cheap because they are not already there. "I stood in the queue all day. What's your excuse?" George might as well be honest.

"The doctor said I wasn't fit, something to do with my chest." Woods comes over to him, and his stride is not at all bad, he grips the railings as the *Kestrel* rolls to the side. Despite his disability, he's more secure than George.

"You'll be better down in the messroom, get some rest before we get to the fishing ground. It'll be dinner soon." George doesn't feel like eating at all.

"I'd just throw it up," says George. Woods knows that the best way to conquer this sea sickness is to find something else to occupy the mind.

"You know there's no point worrying," says Woods. "I mean, if your time's up... there's not a lot you can do about it. This is just a trawler against an ocean of water that never stops rolling." It's a little profound for him to say this. He is trying to distil fatalism into a sentence. Woods wants to be as good a man as his father, but he hasn't had much practise.

"You know just the right thing to say to make a fella feel better. I'm not afraid of dying, I just don't like the feeling of the waves," answers George. He does not yet quite understand that the man is trying to help him.

"Have you ever seen a U-boat?" asks Woods. "A bloke at breakfast said the North Sea's crawling with them." They have both heard about these brand-new weapons that the Imperial German Navy use. They are capable of travelling deep under the water where they can't be spotted, George saw a poster at a news stand and he imagines them, slippery and grey like a dolphin under the water with their torpedoes ready to fire. He had not thought of this when he stepped on board the *Kestrel*. George shakes his head:

"Have you?"

"Not yet, thank God. They sink trawlers for fun," says Woods. "That's why we're going up over the top of Scotland and into the Irish Sea. Skipper Williams isn't a fool. We'll be a long way from the war, mate." It's unusual for Woods to find himself in a situation where he is more knowledgeable than someone else. On the *Kestrel*, even little Jack has been at sea more times than he has, but in this mousey haired man from Cottingham, he finds someone who, out here at least, is weaker than he is. Some men might like to punch down as others have done to them, but that's not how Woods behaves, he's more like his father was.

"You'll fall in love with her," he says.

"Who?"

"The ship." George can't imagine this will be true. "The *Kestrel* is a rust bucket, aye, but she'll keep us all alive all the way there and back, you'll see. You'll fall in love with her." George still can't see it. He retches again but there's nothing in his stomach to come out. His eyes water. He wipes his face with his sleeve.

"When will I start to feel better?"

"Depends. It's much worse if you keep your mind on it. My old man said you just carry on and pretend you don't care, and in the end, you don't. You only get to choose how you

47

deal with stuff—you don't get to choose what happens."

"He said that about feeling seasick, did he?"

"It works for lots of other things too." Tommy Woods should know. It sometimes works for the foot he lost as well.

Below deck is the messroom just off the galley. It's warm after being outside and the smoke hurts George's eyes as he takes a seat. Apart from the skipper who will be up on the bridge, the crew sit bunched up on benches attached to the bulkheads and the tables are bolted to the floor. It stinks of sweat, fish, and cooking oil.

George sits on the end next to Woods. He gets his first sight of the fat cook who brings through a full plate of sausages that he sets on the table next to a big plate of chips. The lads are serving themselves with spoons, there's Big Billy, Peter Everett and the young lad, Jack. John Grace is right at the end with his pale, silent face like stone. The cook emerges again and sets down the same serving of two plates of sausages and chips in front of Woods and George, his nails are black with muck and he wears a vest over his pallid, sweaty body. Cooper, the filthy trimmer, is already slurping on a tin mug of tea in the corner but hasn't taken off his blackened cap. The cook is called Stout, and now he's delivered the food he leans in the doorway for a chat with the crew while he smokes.

"You're a big bastard," he says as he points to Billy. People usually single him out because of this. God knows why. It is sometimes the reason he belts them. Billy keeps chewing sausages as the cook looks at him, his lack of response should be enough warning. "This'll be a piss easy trip," continues the cook, "around to Ireland and back, not nearly as bastard cold as going up to Iceland." He's got a foul mouth. Woods loads his plate with sausages and chips and so does George. Nobody else is up for chatting, just the cook, like he's the owner of some greasy spoon café.

"This your first time at sea is it, son?" he calls to George.

"Aye," his response is flat and cold. It's meant to explain to the cook that he's not in a chatty mood either. Stout takes a pull on his cigarette and blows it out into the little room. There's the smacking of lips as the men eat and the *Kestrel* rocks to one side on the waves below.

"It's gonna be a right trip with you lot," says the cook. He's sarcastic, but without any element of humour.

"What do you mean by that?" asks Woods.

"It'll be all fun and games." He's taking the piss. "I mean you're not exactly full of character, are you? I'm just lucky we've got Young Jack here." He grins and shows his blackened back teeth. "I'll be coming for you in the night, Young Jacko, and we can have a little cuddle. I'll show you what real seafaring is about." Although this is meant to be humorous, there's something sick about the way the cook says it with his slippery oily lips and piggy eyes.

"You'll not touch him," says Big Billy as he chomps on one of the low-quality sausages. There is no warmth in the man's voice as he delivers these words out into the little mess room. Big Billy hates bullies more than anything else, and he doesn't see anything funny about what the cook said, he doesn't give a toss that he's a newcomer here either. It's Billy's uncomplicated way of looking at the world that lands him in trouble sometimes, even if he is doing the right thing.

"It was just a bloody joke," says the cook with a snarl forming at the side of his mouth. It wasn't.

"I'll tell you a joke," says Billy, "it's me breaking your jaw and then using your head to put a hole through one of these walls."

"They're called bulkheads," answers the cook in disdain.

"What are?"

"Walls on a ship..." It's just about to kick off. Billy puts his hands on the table in front of him to rise to his full height of six foot three but before he can, there's a gentle arm put out in front of him. It's the first mate, John Grace. He's got a steady way about him.

"There's no fighting on this ship," he whispers to Billy, and just as quickly, he turns to the cook now standing rather than leaning in the doorway to the galley with his nostrils flared. "And you'll not touch this lad. I've heard about you." At this the cook swallows as he looks down into the stern and cold blue eyes of this Scouser who is possibly too old to give him a good hiding even if he wanted to. John Grace does not like bullies either, he's had to deal with a fair few of them over the years, as first mate, he has to nip this in the bud.

"What have you heard about me?" asks Stout.

"That you're a very good cook, and you keep yourself to yourself, and if you don't, someone will put your head through a steel bulkhead." John Grace is not joking but it comes off as funny. The tension is lifted and Billy falls to his sausage and chips while Stout sinks back to his kitchen to clatter about.

Woods was right, when George lets his mind fix on something else, the seasickness seems to get better. Now he comes back to cutting up one of his sausages, he feels the rocking of the *Kestrel* on the waves below him once more.

"He'll spit in all your food now, you know?" says Cooper as he eats chips with his coal-stained fingers. You can't see the eyes for the peak of the filthy cap.

"Good," answers Big Billy with his mouth full.

CHAPTER SIX

George is starting to get used to the rolling of the ocean beneath his feet, as the day passes into late afternoon. He plays a few hands of a card game called brag with Woods and Cooper in the bunk room while Big Billy snores on one of the beds behind. Periodically, Cooper will slip off to the engine room to add more coal to the furnace. Woods explains that there is no fishing to do until they get round the top of Scotland and down into the Irish Sea. George thinks about his mother in the kitchen back at home, now he is not there, she will rail at Sam instead of him.

At just after two, Jack with his rabbit teeth returns from the bridge and explains that it's George's turn up on deck to take the next watch. George fastens up his duffel coat and goes out the bunkroom, up the iron steps and out onto deck. The winter sky is grey with black clouds across the horizon behind; he makes his way along the side of the *Kestrel* and then climbs the ladder up to the bridge above. It's lonely out in the cold and even this short trip to the wheelhouse is terrifying for George, he clings onto the railings as he moves and grips the rungs of the ladder tightly as he climbs.

Inside the wheelhouse, it's warmer than he expected. At the wheel with his bald head and silver hair behind his ears is the first mate, the Scouser, John Grace. He looks back at George who nods hello.

"Take the wheel," says the Scouser as he steps back. George cocks his head.

"You sure? This is my first trip."

"I can see you're not a dickhead," says Grace. "There's nothing to crash into and I'll be right here. The sea's as flat as a pancake. You see the compass dial reading 020? That's our heading, 020 degrees. Make sure you keep it there. It's a piece of piss." The man has a serious tone. George steps up and puts his hand on the wheel that controls the rudder behind them at the bottom of the ship. Below his feet he can feel the rumble of the steam engine. The furnace heats the boiler and drives pistons that spin the propellor down in the dark North Sea under them. The water is unusually calm and though the *Kestrel* is by no means level, she is not rocking like she did as they passed Spurn Point a while back.

"I also need a word," says the Scouser. George knows this type of man; his father was one before he cleared off. They don't say anything unless they need to and there's no requirement for any chit-chat. "Did you not sign up for the army?"

"The doctor said I wasn't fit. That's why I'm here."

"None of the crew on this ship are fit, son. You and that Billy seem like the only ones who could scratch your arse apart from Young Jack, and he's thirteen. Cooper stinks to high heaven, Peter Everett, our engineer, shivers like a shitting dog, Woods is lame, I'm in my sixties, Skipper Williams is older than me."

"What are you saying?"

"I'm sounding you out to see if you're someone I can trust."

"Wouldn't do much good for me to say yes, would it? Anyone who you can't trust wouldn't tell you so." This is overly wordy for George.

"You can tell a lot about a man by what he doesn't say, and what he does. Like the fact that you haven't taken your eyes off the sea in front all the time you've been holding that wheel." George shrugs:

"That's how you drive a carriage."

"That's how you sail a steam trawler too." The sky in front is moving towards late afternoon. It will be dark within the hour, and as they move further north the night will fall faster. "We're just south of Scarborough Bay now, you do know what happened there, don't you?"

"Of course." Everyone knows what happened, it's been a

rallying call for conscription ever since. Mid December last year, three German warships melted out of the North Sea fog and, at eight o'clock Wednesday morning they pounded the castle and the town. There was nothing there to stop them. The heavy shells shattered castle walls, blew out shop fronts, killed a post man and a boy scout, and when they were done, the German ships turned and sailed away. It galvanized anger. George remembers his mam going on about it after she'd read the story in the Daily Mail Newspaper. John Grace moves closer to him:

"The Germans mean business, son. The faster the fishroom is full, the better. Skipper Williams feels the same way." Grace needs to repay that gambling debt, and every day that he delays the bill gets bigger—thirty days around the top of Scotland to the Irish Sea will be too long a trip. "This crew's not put together for the sort of journey the Humber Steam Trawling Company wants us to make. It'll take a fierce lot of sailing to get around the coast of Scotland and back with this lot. Seems to the skipper and me, that a much better idea would be to cut out into the north towards Iceland. We'll shoot the trawl off, fill her up and head home." George does not know what this really means, but he has a fair idea. First mate John Grace wants to stray out into the ocean and fill the *Kestrel* up with fish rather than sailing round to Ireland as he's been asked.

"What do you need from me?" asks George.

"I want to make sure you and that Big Billy of yours don't give us any shite."

"He's not my mate, I only met him this morning."

"He's a deckie learner, you two are in this together."

"I'm not here to cause trouble but I can't vouch for him." Grace can see already that Billy is a hothead and a fighter. This is great if he is on your side. He was hoping George could control him, seems like he can't.

Out the corner of his eyes, John Grace senses movement

53

on the ocean to the right, he turns. Through the little window on the bridge and coming up on the starboard side is another ship, much bigger than the *Kestrel*. It's British. It seems to have come out of nowhere. Across the bow and written in big white letters is the name *H62 Magnificent*. Grace steps up to move George out the way, he cranks the handle on the ship's telegraph round to slow, this will relay the message to Peter Everett in the engine room. Once he's done this, he opens the door to the cold sky, leans out, and rings the ship's big brass bell with two deep clangs. It will tell the rest of the crew that something is happening. Off the starboard of the *Kestrel*, the *Magnificent* is pulling up and slowing down as well.

"Who's this then?" asks George. Grace keeps the *Kestrel* steady in the water as the other vessel comes alongside. She seems to have melted out of the cloud grey ocean.

"The *Magnificent*, it was a trawler like we are not so long back. It's been requisitioned by the army. See that six-pound gun on the bow." George looks to the huge weapon bolted to the front of the ship and there are two men standing on the side dressed in trawlerman gear but with Admiralty hats. "It's a mine sweeper," he says. John Grace points behind the big trawler to the mid distance. "There's the other one," he says.

"The other what?" asks George. He can see there is another vessel behind the *Magnificent* of a similar size in the distance.

"There're two mine sweepers—that's how they do it."

"What will they want?"

"Probably a chat."

It's just after three o'clock and the wind off the North Sea is not strong but it still has barbs of cold within it. Skipper Williams is on deck with his duffle coat buttoned up to his neck and his thin face pale with a red nose. He looks withered as he grips onto the handrail of the *Kestrel* and shouts across to the skipper and the first mate of the *Magnificent*. If the seas were rough, you wouldn't be able to get ships this close to each other to speak. This is a social call, for both men.

The skipper of the *Magnificent* is tall with a black handlebar moustache and dark eyes. Like the first mate behind him, he's wearing a cap with the mine clearance service badge worn slightly off centre above the peak. They're part of the Admiralty, but then they're not part of it, somehow. These men won't take orders from a Royal Navy captain but they will follow Skipper Edgar here who's a Hessle Road lad from Wassand Street. Fishermen don't do well being told what to do anyway, especially by someone who has less experience of the sea than they do. Williams knows this Skipper Edgar. Twenty-five years ago, he was a fifteen-year-old deckie learner on board a trawler he commanded named the *Oberon*.

"Now then Egsy," calls Williams over the ten yards of water. Nobody else would be able to call him this.

"Skipper Edgar to you, Williams," shouts the skipper. The waves are not so bad, but both boats rock on the waters ten miles out from Scarborough Bay as they keep pace. "I thought you'd be dead by now," This makes Williams smile. He likes this mean humour.

"I'll be sailing longer than you, Egsy, if you're sweeping for German mines, bits of your arse'll be washing up on Hornsea beach for months." Edgar should not try to be clever with Skipper Williams; the man has honed the skill of being a bastard over many years and thousands of miles. Skipper Edgar runs his eyes over the little trawler called the *Kestrel*, he sees the pitch black funnel with smoke belching from it, the rusted rivets along the sides and notes the men on board. Behind Skipper Williams, is a fat man in his sixties easily, and peering out from the open door of the wheelhouse is a thirteen-year old kid who looks like he could be out of a Dickens novel with his hollow eyes and ripped trousers.

"Where you headed?" asks Edgar.

"Around the Orkneys and into the Irish Sea."

"You'll stick to the cleared lanes," shouts Edgar. "The North Sea's teeming with U-boats and mines."

"We haven't come across anything yet."

"When you do there'll be nothing left of you."

"I've been at this game too long to let any of that worry me, Egsy. You and your fancy pants caps and badges can have all the fun you like sailing up and down here—some of us have got fish to catch."

Just as Edgar did, Williams casts his eyes over the *Magnificent*. Edgar's face is pale and stern as he stands with his boot up on the port side, behind him there are trawlermen with Admiralty caps and roll-necked sweaters under thick coats, a long haired Jack Russell comes to stand next to his skipper and it examines the boat keeping pace alongside with keen eyes. It's a converted trawler alright. Williams knows the work these men will be doing, and there'll be no glory of the open sea for them, theirs will be monotony. Up there on the bridge with binoculars will be two lookout lads scanning the seas around them for anything that looks like it could be a mine. Once they spot something, dead slow, the *Magnificent* and the vessel they're working with will drag a wire between them through the North Sea to try and hook it up. It is boring, dangerous work, if you miss something—and everyone does once in a while, you could all be dead. Williams does not envy Edgar here but if these brave men did not do this, nothing would move on the North Sea for fear of being sunk.

"I'd ask you on board for a nip of something, Skipper," calls Edgar, "but we're on patrol. How many crew have you got there?"

"Nine of us." Edgar grimaces. It's an unlucky number but then he knows from experience that Skipper Williams does not worry about superstitions.

"Any munitions?" Skipper Williams shakes his head.

"This is a trawler, Egsy."

"Not even a rifle?" Skipper Williams shrugs his shoulders.

Edgar gives a quick order to his first mate behind and the man disappears off into the *Magnificent*. He returns a moment later with a long brown rifle and a box of bullets.

"We don't need it," says Williams. "The sea hasn't got me in all these years, Egsy, she's not going to get me now."

"It's not the sea I'm worried about, Skipper," he calls back. John Grace sees the gun in the first mate of the *Magnificent's* hands and he steps up to catch it.

"We don't need your bloody gun on board this ship," repeats Williams. John Grace does not agree. He's not sure any of them could take on Big Billy if the lad gets nasty, so the rifle might be a good antidote to this.

"I'll look after it," he calls over at the *Magnificent* skipper as he looks up to the wheelhouse where Young Jack keeps the *Kestrel* steady. The boats edge closer and John Grace leans over and takes hold of the rifle. He swings the strap over his shoulder and collects the box of bullets, they are heavier than they look. The conversation is almost over between these vessels, the sky above is darkening and they've said all they have to say.

"Keep to the coast. Once you get round Scotland, you should be fine, but don't put out to sea proper. You'll get sunk by a U-boat or a mine." Skipper Edgar says this with authority, but he's got no idea if it's true. Noone knows quite how many U-boats the Kaiser has got in the dark sea or how many mines there are either. Skipper Williams gives a wry smile.

"You just worry about your lot, Egsy, let me worry about mine." Skipper Edgar looks over his shoulder to the bridge and makes a circle motion with his finger in the air. The *Magnificent* disengages from the *Kestrel* as the helmsman on the bridge edges her away starboard and towards the coast. The men standing on each boat are motionless as they get further away from each other. Skipper Edgar thinks about giving a half arsed, ironic salute, but he knows the trawler men would not appreciate it.

As the *Kestrel* pulls away and the darkness of the late afternoon comes down on the deck of the *Magnificent*, the first mate turns to Skipper Edgar:

"They shouldn't be out fishing," he mutters. Edgar does not take his eyes off the *Kestrel* as it banks to the port side and off into the rough North Sea waves. The men who five minutes previous stood in front of him are now becoming smaller in the distance as Skipper Williams clambers back up to the bridge in the worsening sea.

"Williams was the first skipper I worked for," says Edgar.

"What was he like?" asks the first mate.

"A bastard, and a pirate as well, but he knows how to sail a trawler and he knows the north water."

"They'll have a powerful long trip up to Scotland and round to Ireland."

"He won't be going that way, kid. He'll be out to sea the first chance he gets because the quicker he can fill up that fishroom, the sooner he can get home and get paid." The first mate blinks in the cold of the grey afternoon, the wind has whipped up from the open sea ahead.

"If he hits a mine, that'll be the end of him." Here on the *Magnificent* they have swept many of these round German mines out of this ocean already. They are huge, studded balls that float from the seabed on weights a few feet under the surface—they are ingenious and cruel. The Magnificent and her sister ship get a good distance away, then the crew explode them with rifles from the deck. It would only take one of these in the right place to split the *Kestrel* in half.

"He'll head north, I know he will."

"He's a bloody fool if he tries. He'll be lucky to get away with his life," says the first mate.

"That's just it," answers Skipper Edgar as he turns away from the sea. "He's the only skipper I've ever known that doesn't give a toss about luck, and he's not afraid of the sea neither. It's like he wants her to have him."

CHAPTER SEVEN

Under the wheelhouse of the *Kestrel* is a little chartroom where the skipper keeps his maps. There's a table fixed in the centre with benches secured to the bulkhead and a map cabinet in the corner. John Grace sits at one side of the table and Skipper Williams at the other. It's not for the rest of the crew. Woods stands leaning on the closed door to the deck. It's half eight in the morning, the skipper and Grace have tin mugs of tea. On the floor under the table is the skipper's blue cat with its tail waving behind it like a cobra doing the snake dance.

"Where are we sailing?" asks Woods. He's already realised that the *Kestrel* is not following the coast. Any sailor with eyes in his head can see from the sun, hidden behind the clouds, that they are heading dead north.

"I told Grace here that you were as sharp as your father," says the skipper. "If not for that screwed up foot of yours, you'd have made a fine trawlerman." This isn't meant to be either kind-hearted or cruel, it's just the truth.

"I'm a fine trawlerman anyway," says Woods, although he doesn't believe this. John Grace looks up to the young man at the door:

"The skipper here is sailing us south of Iceland. We'll fill up with fish and then turn around, we should be back within a fortnight, three weeks max." This is what the Scouser hopes, for his debt grows bigger by the day. Woods examines Grace's serious stare and then looks to Skipper Williams, the skin on the old man's face is leathery and there's a look of steel in his blue eyes. Woods could mention the war and the mines and the U-boats but there is little point, these men will have made their mind up about the destination of the trawler already.

"In case you're worried, Woods," says the skipper. "It's a bloody big sea out there, and all that shite you've heard about floating bombs and Germans in underwater boats is nowt to do with us. That Peter Everett will tell you he got sunk by a torpedo, but he was in a battleship. Do you really think they'd waste a bullet like that on a boat like this?"

"I wasn't worried," says Woods with a shrug.

"Is it your first time as a bosun, Woods?" This is John Grace. His light Scouse accent is old style and smooth rather than rasping.

"Aye."

"I want it all clean out there. Once we get to the grounds, we'll be at it hard for seven days or more, so this is your time to get everything ready." Grace does not have to say this because it's the bosun's job to look after everything on deck anyway. It's a way for the Scouser to divert attention from the war and the mines and the U-boat threat. "I need those two deckie learners trained up as well. You don't have to explain the finer details of trawling but let them know how the boat works and what's expected of them."

"What do you think of the new lads?" asks the skipper to Woods.

"George seems ok. Billy's a nutter."

"What kind of nutter?" asks John Grace.

"Does it matter?" replies the skipper. "This is a Hull trawler. You have to be a bloody nutter to do the job." Neither man responds to this but there's some truth in it.

"I'll keep my eye on him," says Woods.

"What will you do if he gets out of hand?" He shrugs his shoulders again. Grace's stare is withering and Woods is conscious, as he always is, that he is a cripple among real men of the sea, and that he is only here now because those more able than he, are away at war.

"You don't make people behave by threatening them, Grace, that's what coppers do," says the skipper. Williams has a cruel wisdom to him. "I think Woods has done well so far, there's a lot of his father in him, he talks to people—that's how you manage folk and that's how you deal with lads at sea.

He's good at it."

"I'm all for peace skipper," says Grace, "but if that big bastard starts swinging his fists, then I'll put an end to it." He points to the rifle laid on the cabinet opposite. Skipper Williams blows air out his mouth to suggests Grace is full of shite.

"There'll be no need for that," he whispers. The blue cat jumps to the bench next to the skipper and pads onto his lap where it sits down. The yellow eyes examine Woods as he leans on the doorframe. "I need a word with you, young Woods. Alone." He gives John Grace a sideways glance and the Scouser stands up. Woods steps out of his way so he can move through the door of the chart room and onto the deck. It leaves the younger man standing in front of Skipper Williams.

"Sit down, lad," says the older man. Woods takes a seat on the bench and feels nervous with the skipper and his big, yellow eyed blue cat staring at him. "How many trips have you been on?" Woods frowns in thought. This is his first job as a bosun, but he's been to sea a good number of times.

"Six trips, Skipper," he answers.

"I knew your father," says Williams. "He was a good sailor and not just because he could work hard, he knew this dark water. He knew how people worked as well; he could talk to them. It's not a gift that I share—that's why I liked having him on ships where I was skipper." Woods knew that his father was a warm man, but this is the first time it has struck him that this was a valuable trait on a fishing boat. "I don't run ships like other skippers do, Woods. I don't go with all this superstitious shite and I'm not afraid of the sea. I don't tell jokes. I don't listen well and I don't suffer fools—that was your father's job. You've got his easy way with other men." The skipper's fingers rub behind the delicate ears of the cat on his lap and it curls its head towards them. Woods is good with people because he likes them. It's not something you can fake, and he likes to ask questions and listen to their answers.

"The lads say that you're not afraid of the sea at all. I've heard it from folk on the shore as well." If this old man is going to be frank, then so is Tommy Woods. Even so, they should not be speaking like this on a Hull trawler. Like boasting, speaking of the sea is the quickest way for something unpleasant to happen to you.

"She took something away from me a long time ago, Woods. I was younger than you are now and I worked the box fleets off Dogger Bank before all this steam. We sailed like proper men do, at the sea's mercy with cloth canvas flapping above. You needed real skill in those days. She sent a swell and a storm across from the east of an early winter morning. I won't bore you with it, kid. I was port side hauling in the net with my Uncle Harold, and a few of us, good steady lads they were. He had a fox terrier called Kip, a real good dog." Skipper William's voice is softer than usual somehow as he explains. He can still remember the morning that it happened as if it were yesterday. He continues:

"There was a storm came upon us right quick, the skipper told us to clear the deck but Harold called up to him that we'd stay topside and get in the net we had hold of. Well, a great wave, the like of which I've never seen since, washed over the ship. The *Laurel* she was called, and the salt water pushed us all backwards with the force." The eyes of the old skipper mist up as he goes back to that freezing morning on the *Laurel*. "When the boat rocked itself right way, we were all still there. I'd clung on to the net, but that little fox-terrier, Kip, had been swept overboard in front of us. My Uncle Harold roared at her in the water to swim, but the sea was up and savage like. He wasn't going to go in after her, but he leaned out over the port side and another of them big waves came crashing down on the *Laurel*, and he was gone."

Williams does not know why he is telling this to Woods. He's not spoken of it before, not to his wife or his daughter or the many men he sailed and fished with over all these years.

"I stood there, and I whispered that if she sent him back, she could have me instead. She could have me now, or in any of the years to come, just as long as she sent him back; but when the boat levelled out again after more of the waves, the skipper ordered us off the deck. Before we could get below, that fox-terrier surfaced alright, and one of the hands got hold of her to pull her on board by the scruff of her neck, but my Uncle Harold was gone under. That was it. It was like she was mocking me, sending back that dog but not my uncle."

Woods can see into the old man for a moment. He can see the bitterness therein that he carries with him even as they sit in the bleak chartroom of the *Kestrel*. Some folk can be broken and grow back, not so Skipper Williams here. It emptied him of trust, and the sense that there was ever any goodness in the world is gone. It hardened him to the man he has been since then.

"The sea took that from me. She knows I'm not afraid of her and that if I was to drown, I'd be with the only man I ever cared for. You know what she's like, kid, she's too cruel to give that to me." Woods is a good listener, and perhaps Williams has softened with age. The old man swallows and comes back to himself, his eyes sharpen and his voice returns to the usual rasp:

"I want you to be everyone's friend, just like your father used to be. That's your job, just the same as it is to keep the deck in good order. If you do it right, we'll catch all the fish we need and be back in Hull in a few weeks. Cock it up, and John Grace will end up shooting some poor bastard. Do you understand?" Woods nods.

"I won't let you down, Skipper." Woods is not sure what he has agreed to do but as he sits there on the bench with the roll of the North Sea under him and his wooden foot at an angle under the table, he feels the heavy weight of responsibility gently rest upon his shoulders. Nobody has trusted poor Tommy Woods before with his gammy, cocked-up foot and his limp, but here he is, a bosun and a trawlerman, finally.

At the request of Grace, Woods shows the two deckie learners around the ship before they get to the grounds. It gives them all something to do and it'll make it much quicker if these two men know their duties before they start fishing. Big Billy considers the water around him, they can no longer see land and the sky is a dull, monotone grey. Woods has never been in a position to explain much to anyone before, but it suits him and not in a preachy way. This approach works well with Big Billy:

"See these girders sticking out the side of the boat?" he explains. "They're gallows. We shoot a net into the water and drag it behind the ship, every couple of hours we pull it onboard with the winch, haul it over the side by hand and empty it before we shoot it again." For brevity, Woods has simplified a process that has been refined to an artform by generations of fishermen before him. As Grace told him to, he won't bother with the terms and delicate nature of the net, how otter boards keep it open as it rolls along the seabed, how the winch man must be careful not to taffle up the warp cables, how the skipper will position the boat sideways and how the waves make the job of hauling the net onboard easier. Woods can see George examining the winch and the equipment with keen eyes, Big Billy is looking back over the stern at the couple of seagulls that flap in the wake.

"How long till we start fishing?" asks George.

"A day or two," says Woods. He won't explain to these men that they aren't going up and round to Ireland after all. George won't realise what's happening, and Big Billy doesn't look like he would be bothered either way. The smaller man seems over the seasickness already but he still looks pale.

The *Kestrel* sails.

Skipper Williams is alone in the wheelhouse, and the round

eyes of his English blue cat look out of the windows at the cold sea drifting by. Stout chops carrots and spuds in the tiny galley kitchen. Cooper makes sure the fuel in the coal room is flat and even, so the ship stays level and, shivering as he adjusts the throttle that drives the propellor shaft, Peter Everett keeps the engine powering the ship forwards.

The winter sea is rough around them but the crew are busy. Young Jack inspects and fixes nets with Woods. They wear big waterproof jackets, caps, and wellington boots against the spray from the sea and the bitter rain. Billy and George are considered deckie learners, those not skilled enough to do even the most basic job connected with fishing. They're made to wash and scrub the deck down with stiff brushes. The *Kestrel* rolls and falls on the waves and with each pitch and rise, George feels his stomach copy the movement. The weather is getting worse.

They break for tea mid-morning and sitting in the messroom with one of the tin mugs in his hand, George watches a thick fog roll over the *Kestrel* from the icy sea. He is glad he is inside because a blanket of grey cloud comes in. Like dark cotton wool, it envelops them completely. In the messroom the electric lights under grates on the wall now glow bright against the dark morning. He feels the boat slow as the fog rolls over them. The wind picks up from the east, and the trawler dips suddenly downwards then crests upwards as it rides a huge wave that has seemingly come from nowhere. Freezing rain begins to fall outside.

George thought he had got used to sailing already, but this movement makes his stomach roll inside him. Stout appears at the doorway to the kitchen and scratches his stomach while he looks out through the tiny window opposite—they have hit a storm already and the boat lurches to the side and pitches forward. Stout has been in hundreds of storms, he can sleep through them even. Like a lot of seamen, his body is so used to the ocean's movements that leaning against the bulkhead to stop himself falling over, is as common to him as frying an egg or wiping his fat arse.

"She's come in fast," he says, meaning the storm, and not particularly to anyone as he peers out to the grey sky darkening. George puts his hand to his head in fatigue. It feels like this trip is going to get much worse.

Young Jack throws open the messroom door and steps in, sea spray and wind blast through into the room, his coat and hat run with water. Rain hammers the toughened glass of the window and the ship pitches to the port side. The young lad's face is concerned:

"Woods has got himself stuck," he calls as he gets through the door. "He's got his wooden foot jammed in the bottom of the winch. I'm not strong enough to pull him out."

Up in the wheelhouse, Skipper Williams is turning the trawler into the bad weather while the blue cat, unworried behind the glass, watches huge waves roll out of the sea at them. The door to the wheelhouse opens and icy rain and seawater spray inside, John Grace has hauled himself up the ladder and he comes through, already drenched. He pulls the door closed behind him.

"I didn't see that coming," he mutters.

"You never do with the big ones," says the skipper. Grace removes his wet cap and shakes it out onto the dull steel under their feet. Skipper Williams leans forward and narrows his eyes down onto the deck. There's the black shape of a trawlerman just to the side of the winch, the rain on the window obscures his vision. "Who's that daft twat still on deck?" he calls. Grace steps forwards to get a better look.

"I dunno, Skipper,"

"Get him inside before he gets washed overboard," he growls. "I need all the bloody hands I can get to fill this fishroom." Williams's first instinct is not so much the man himself, but his abilities as a worker. Grace puts the wet cap on his head once more and opens the door to the wind and the rain of the north water. He must climb down the ladder to get back onto the deck—it's not hard in normal conditions, but he is sixty-four years old and his body isn't what it once was. He leans out and bellows down at the figure next to the trawl winch fifty yards ahead through the freezing, driving rain.

"Woods!" He sees the figure stand and then drop back down. Grace curses under his breath. He will have to go and help the man. Perhaps he should have stayed in Hull after all, even with that debt hanging over him he'd live, out here he might get swept off into the water as he goes to the lad's aid. Grace is a brave man in so much that he will not see another person die, but he doesn't do it with a glad heart. He turns to begin the descent down the ladder and sees two figures emerge from the messroom. One is the tall shape of Big Billy, the other is the gaunt looking George, they are making their way down the *Kestrel* holding onto the guard rails as she banks and dips. Neither of them is wearing a jacket meaning they have either come onto deck in an emergency or they don't expect to stay out.

"Woods is down there," he yells into the wind but he can see that's where they are headed. Grace is about to close the wheelhouse door when he hears George call up to him from below:

"He's got his foot trapped." John Grace tuts as he hears this. He closes the door behind him and the world is suddenly silent once more in the wheelhouse.

"Woods has got his bloody foot stuck in something," he repeats in disgust to the skipper. "He shouldn't be on the ship. We shouldn't be fishing with men like that." Skipper Williams does not take his eyes off the huge waves that come rolling at them out of the grey rain. It is best to steer into them. He does not know the *Kestrel* well enough to judge how well she will deal with this storm, but he'll find out. You only get through problems by facing them.

"Did you hear me?" asks Grace. "That man's a liability."

"He's fitter than you are," says the skipper.

Woods has got his foot stuck in the space next to the trawl winch. It's his wooden foot. He's unlucky. Something like this was bound to happen. In the rain and the pitching of the vessel, his slippery hands go to pull the boot free from the hole it's been jammed into. The foot is strapped to his leg tight and the space has his ankle gripped. The *Kestrel* rolls down and to the starboard side and he feels the pain as his leg takes the strain. Freezing water washes over him; the ice goes down the back of his neck. His heart pounds at the shock of it as he struggles to make sense of if his body is upwards or spinning. Through gritted teeth, Woods tries to get a better look at his foot trapped in the space. Another wave washes over him. He cannot quite see where he is. Freezing saltwater is in his mouth and eyes, the pressure on his ankle is mounting. If he breaks his leg, it will be worse than getting washed overboard.

Woods feels disappointment pressing heavy on the walls of his chest, for here he is, a cripple who promised he would be fine on a fishing trawler, trapped like a child. He will try to get himself out of this but his hands are already stiffening up in the cold of the north water. It might be better if he gets washed off, for if he does not return to Hull with something to show for himself, there is no point in returning at all—his mother told him so. Like all his life, he has been a failure.

The *Kestrel* rises on a great wave from below her, spray, and ice water wash over the bow and across Tommy Woods trapped next to the trawl winch. The ship rises high into the air and then dips, nose first over this great wave and down, driving into a white cliff that engulfs the front end of her.

George reaches Woods first as the water runs off the deck and back into the sea through the railings and scuppers. He looks down to see the crumpled boot at the wrong angle next to the trawl winch, gives it a tug and Woods shakes his head in pain. Another wave crashes over the both of them. Big Billy appears and appraises the situation. He reaches down into the hole with both hands to pull out the foot. Back in Etton, Billy has freed plenty of cows with their hooves stuck in cattle grids, you have to be firm to get the job done. The *Kestrel* rolls to one side and there's a crack as Billy tugs the foot free from the hole. Woods is about to slide backwards down the deck as the ship rises but George grabs him by the slippery jacket and hauls him to his feet while Billy takes the other arm. Like they are bringing a drunkard back from the ale house, they stagger down the side of the ship as it banks and dips. From the wheelhouse, John Grace watches the men.

"He shouldn't be on this ship," he mutters.

"It's not right that a pair of deckie learners had to fetch that lad back inside, neither" says Skipper Williams, "why didn't you help?"

"I'm not as young as I was."

"Maybe it's you that shouldn't be on this ship." Grace sneers back at the old man holding the wheel.

In the messroom, Woods is pale. They have set him down on the bench attached to the bulkhead. Young Jack has managed to remove his false foot by unclipping the straps that held it in place up his legs and below his knee. Outside, rain hammers the windows and the sky is grey while the ship still pitches and rolls on great swells from the north water below. George picks up the prosthetic boot, there's a big s shaped hook jammed in the sole. He holds the piece of curved metal up to Woods after pulling it out.

"A net hook," says Jack.

"If that was your real foot you'd not be walking," adds George. Woods manages a weak smile. This is true. Trawlerman use these big hooks to hang the nets while they mend holes, one must have fallen down into the space in front of the trawl winch.

"You're lucky," says Jack. Woods has never been called this before. Perhaps today he has been. Stout stands in the doorway to his kitchen with a sarcastic grin on his greasy face.

"It's not the first accident you've had is it, Woods?" he says. "I heard you fell into a fish room as a lad and that's why they had to chop off your foot." His tone seems happy at another's misfortune. Woods looks back at him and remembers a day he would rather forget, and one that has overshadowed every step he has taken since—literally. "You're clumsy, pal, like a puppet with that wooden foot clunking all over the deck." There is no need for this. It's more bullying than the usual cruel sarcasm these lads use to get through the days. Big Billy stands and steps towards the greasy cook, he is a good few inches taller than him.

"I don't like the way you sound," says Billy.

"Is that so? You don't have to listen when I'm speaking." Stout cocks his head, without Grace here he is going to have to stand up to this farm lad, for his pride's sake.

"Your stupid voice makes me want to belt you." What Stout doesn't know is that Big Billy is restraining himself. Ordinarily if he thinks someone deserves a slap, he'll give them one. There are a number of factors that have stopped him hitting Stout so far, the fact that he's in unfamiliar surroundings and just over a week ago, he murdered his own father in a brawl outside the White Horse pub in Beverley.

"I'm not scared of you," whispers Stout even though he is. Big Billy moves closer yet. He will say one more line and if the man responds, he'll do something nasty.

"He's not worth it, Billy," this is Woods. He does not want a fight breaking out, the skipper has tasked him with keeping these men from each other's throats after all. "Who'll do our tea if you crack him one, you'll probably kill him." Woods says this more to frighten Stout into submission. Billy turns to look at the men in the messroom around him. George is taking off his wet jumper. Woods is on the bench with his feet splayed out in front of him. Young Jack blinks up at him from under his bowl haircut with those rabbit teeth. The word kill has frightened Billy and he steps back. Stout retreats into the kitchen and there's the sound of pots and pans banging as if he's more important than he is.

The *Kestrel* rolls to one side as she rides another wave from under the ocean. George peers out the window with the rain hammering on the glass, he can see the lights of another ship far away out of the storm. Jack appears at his side and places his hand on the glass as he looks at the ship in the mid-distance.

"It's a cruiser," he whispers. George wonders how his eyesight is that good. "There's another one behind her, see." Jack points out into the moving horizon. The *Kestrel* rocks backwards so all they can see is grey cloud above, and then back down into the waves. "It'll be the Great Fleet," says Jack, and there's a sense of awe in his high-pitched voice. "It will be the Great Fleet, won't it, Woods?" he calls over his shoulder.

"Aye, I should think so." Billy sits down. His face looks washed out.

"What's the Great Fleet?" he asks. Young Jack explains in a breathless voice.

"It's a blockade, all the way from the north of Scotland here to Norway. Cruisers and warships, they're stopping the Germans getting in and getting out. First Mate Grace says that's how we'll win the war, we'll starve the Kaiser. He'll get nothing through from the rest of the world if we cut him off here and south, near Dover." Woods looks out of the window again at the cruiser lights in the distance. It's much bigger than the *Kestrel* and seems more at ease on the waves from this far away.

"The skipper won't get too close to them, kid," says Woods. "Not in this weather." From the bow end of the ship there's a shrill piping sound, this is the whistle from the steam engine. It will be Skipper Williams signalling to the cruiser as

71

they pass in the storm. It's as close as the ships will get.

Jack watches from the window and George goes to sit down; he is too tired to worry about how the boat is rocking with the storm outside. The electric light on the wall flickers out and the room is dark suddenly. They hear Stout swear from the kitchen, and for a moment, George gets a sense of where he is, truly. They are out here rolling on the waves under the great and wide sky as powerless as any sailor has ever been against the might of the ocean. He understands a little of what Woods explained to him when he first came aboard the *Kestrel*, that his life or his death is out of his control. The sea will have him if she so wants, like she'll have all the crew— there's no point worrying, you'll never know till it happens anyway.

"Thanks for coming out to get me," says Woods. "I owe you two lads." Billy likes to help people. George did it because it was the right thing to do, like his mam taught him. Jack gasps in awe as he catches glimpses of the battle cruiser between the movement of the *Kestrel* on the heavy waves.

"How long will this last?" says George, and at once realises that this shows he hasn't learned anything. The sea will do whatever she likes. Woods sighs:

"A good sailor is never impatient." He feels safe with these two deckie learners and Young Jack, as if he can say what he likes and they won't take the piss. "You don't get to choose when the wind stops or if it blows. Like I said about your seasickness, if you pretend you don't care about it, eventually you don't. The only choice you've got is how you deal with it."

CHAPTER EIGHT

This is the *SM U-19*. The SM stands for Seiner Majestät and means 'his majesty's' in English. She's a German U-boat and there's a lookout alone on the bridge with binoculars to his blue eyes in goggles. He's dressed in a heavy overcoat and his dark Kaiserliche Marine cap covers the tightly cropped blonde hair. His mouth is pencil thin because of the cold and spray from the ocean. They take it in turns to be lookout and whatever the soldiers and housewives back in Germany think, U-boats spend most of their time on the surface. In five minutes, Joseph Krieger, the captain, will take over. They have been three weeks at sea on patrol. They are on their way home.

The keel of the *SM U-19* was set down in October 1911 at Danzig. In peacetime she hunted the Russian coast to the north and all the way as far as the Mediterranean under the direction of a man of sailing experience and honour named, Raimond Weisbach. Until three months ago, Krieger served under him, first as a torpedo officer and then as his second in command. Weisbach was old even before the *U-19* was built, and the rigors of life in a tiny U-boat exacerbated his arthritis and lung condition. He had a grey schnauzer named Rene, a beautiful thing with dark, expressive eyes, a grey beard, and a temper. It ran up and down the U-boat, shat in the engine room, begged for food when the men ate, and had a high-pitched bark if it thought there was a rat behind the electric batteries or the diesel cans. Weisbach stood down and the man who knew the *U-19* better than anyone, is Krieger himself—that's why he's the captain. His first order was 'no animals'.

Krieger was repulsed by the smell when he stepped on board three weeks ago, like he always is. There's the ingrained stink of men crammed together, hot and humid diesel from the engine and chlorine coming off the electric batteries. You do get used to it.

The *U-19* is two hundred feet long and twelve feet in

73

diameter on the outside. Inside it feels tiny on account of the ballast tanks that help it dive and rise in the water. Sweat runs down the bulkheads. Loose rivets let in trickles of water. Exposed wires and cables run behind buttons and wheels that control the pumps and ballast tanks. At the fore are the torpedo tubes and at the start of a patrol, spare torpedoes are kept there as well. Like mines, these U-boats have changed the nature of naval warfare. Not so long ago, the biggest ships with the heaviest guns ruled the waves, but today, the threat of the unseen mine or U-boat keeps big dreadnoughts safe in port for fear that either could send them to the bottom of the ocean. Life on a U-boat is not without its dangers. The *SM U-15* was rammed and sunk by *HMS Birmingham* last August, so too was the *SM U-20*, struck by a British ship and sunk in November. *SM U-12* hit a mine, so they heard. *SM U-11* was lost at sea, and nobody knows why.

The weather and sea are rough outside, so Krieger has ordered the hatches to the world above to be closed, for the *U-19* cannot afford to have too much water inside her. There are twenty-nine men on board and the twin diesel engines hum as she cuts through the ocean in the darkness. These boats only dive when they don't want to be spotted and they can't do it for long. Up on the bridge outside in that heavy coat, is the first mate, on watch—it's freezing cold out there in the wind, but the U-boat is only as effective as what it can see and there must be a man or two up there at all times.

Krieger stands at the bottom of the ladder and throws a heavy coat over his shoulders, puts on thick leather gloves, and pulls his white cap over his dark hair. He's five foot seven and stocky, with a smile that he reserves for friends, and cold brown eyes for everyone else. Krieger is apt to let other men speak and chatter away while he observes, but when he gives an order, he is sure of himself and he expects it done quickly. Nero stands looking up at him with an expectant face and her little paws clacking on the metal floor in excitement.

"You're not coming up," he says to the black and tan dog. "You'll get washed overboard." He said no animals. This is a vessel for war after all and nobody warmed to the schnauzer that old Weisbach had anyway. Nero here is the engineer's animal and she's a miniature pinscher, a zwergpinscher which means little biter. She's got a fine temperament, doesn't moult, and is small enough to never get in the way. Felix says that he got her from one of the whores back at Wilhelmshaven, the madam wouldn't let her keep Nero in the whorehouse so he offered to look after the little dog, permanently. The crew have taken to her as well. She is regal, like Anubis with her black ears pointing straight up. Felix smuggled her on board and she is a gentle soul. Krieger is glad she is here.

"Sorry, girl," he says. Krieger doesn't have to do this, understand, he's the captain. He could have any of the younger less experienced men go out there and stand in the wind and freezing spray of the North Sea, but he will not have any man do a job that he is not prepared to do himself. Like Weisbach taught him, he leads by example and so he will take his turn on watch like everyone else. Once dressed, he loops binoculars over his head and he climbs up the steel ladder to the hatch where he turns the round handle and pushes it open to the world outside.

Krieger is quick as he gets out onto the bridge above, and the crewman he replaces is just as swift to get out of the cold and back into the U-boat below. They must minimise how much moisture gets inside, so do not exchange pleasantries as they switch places—there's no point, like all the men on the *U-19*, they have been closer to each other than brothers already. Krieger grabs onto the railings, giving the man space to move down the ladder and close the hatch, and then, he is all alone in the grey winter of the ocean.

There's peace in the solitude, and the fresh morning sea air is welcome at first until the cold starts to bite properly. He surveys the water around him and narrows his eyes at the horizon as the *U-19* cuts through the choppy waters out of the Atlantic towards the North Sea. Krieger is on the lookout for anything that moves. This is how they hunt.

The war started in July last year, and has moved quickly onto many fronts, not least here on the sea. The *SM U-19* is cutting edge technology and part of the evolution within the Kaiser's navy that stretches back to the *U-1*. Every iteration of the machine has got progressively better. The *U-19* has two eight-cylinder diesel motors and a double motor-generator for electric power. Older U-boats used kerosene and were only good enough for a thousand miles before they had to turn back for home, but the *U-19* has a range of twelve thousand miles; she can stay at sea for weeks at a time, and dive for two hours straight at a depth of fifty metres. The U-boats have struck fear into the British and challenged their supremacy on the waters around the world. Since February, the Kaiser has ordered unrestricted war on any allied ships. That means they can sink anything they see, merchants, cargo vessels, trawlers, and row boats if they like.

In September last year, the *U-21*, a newer version of Krieger's vessel, fired a single twenty-inch torpedo at a range of two thousand yards. The lookout on board the *HMS Pathfinder* saw its wake but the ship could not manoeuvre fast enough to evade it. The torpedo struck under the bridge and set off bags of cordite causing a massive secondary explosion. She went down so quickly they couldn't launch the lifeboats. That's what a crew of twenty-nine on a U-boat can do to a two-hundred and seventy foot cruiser.

Krieger and his men have sunk five vessels in this last hunting trip, and they are becoming experts. It's not without its dangers. The lookout on the bridge scans the horizon as they move through the water and as soon as they see anything of note, the *U-19* dives so they are hidden. The diesel engines switch off and the batteries kick in. Underwater there's no way to get rid of the exhaust fumes. Krieger and the first mate take turns checking the periscope to identify the vessel—if it's big and it's armed, they fire a torpedo from the tubes at the front. If it's a fishing or a merchant ship, they get as close as they can and surface. The crew of the *U-19* clamber out onto the deck with rifles and loud shouts and Krieger calls to the skipper of whatever merchant or fishing ship it is. He tells them they have five minutes to collect themselves together, five minutes to board and float the lifeboats, then five minutes to get as far away as they can from their vessel. Krieger is not a monster.

They use the heavy deck gun to blow a hole in the hull, or two if necessary. It's good for morale and target practice as well. The *U-19* used to stay and watch as the ships slowly sank into the dark water, but these days, they are anxious to get away. Krieger looks to the men, and sometimes women in the lifeboats across the choppy sea with their moon faces and wide eyes—at least they have their lives. The captain of the *U-19* has a conscience.

Krieger puts the binoculars to his eyes in the light rain and scans the horizon once again. He turns and leans against the railings as he checks the sea behind and in all directions in a sweep. He trained the men to do just this. The wind is beginning to chill him despite the heavy coat, gloves, and the hat, but there is peace out here somehow, even though the sky is oil painting grey and the metal sides of the U-boat complain against the waves.

Like all good leaders, Krieger did not start out wanting the position or the power. It was duty and circumstance that put him here. In the summer of 1889 when his father died, he, his sisters and his mother moved to the lakes southwest of Berlin, and it was here that Krieger's grandfather taught him how to sail wooden yachts with their flapping sails and long keels to keep them upright. He learned discipline and duty on the bigger sailing vessels, and then went to naval academy in Danzig when he was seventeen.

Krieger is a Christian, like his grandfather. This war is not a thing to be savoured or glorified. It's a duty to be done and a task to be completed so that the world can go back to how it should be. He was stationed at Wilhelmshaven on the North Sea coast and served as a petty officer on naval scouts. The Kaiserliche Marine singled him out to serve on U-boats because he was small, quiet, and worked hard. He spent time under the water on the *U-11* and then the *U-15*. On the *U-21*, in September last year, it was Krieger who gave the order for the torpedo to be loaded. It was he who called down the corridor for the tube to be closed and for it to be fired at *HMS Pathfinder*. It was he who later looked out from the deck when they had surfaced to see the figures in the water, pathetic and floundering, as they drown, bug eyed and open mouthed, thrashing in silence through the loud rush of the wind like they were insects dissolving in solution on the end of a microscope. Krieger will do all the hunting and killing that he has to do, but he will not kill in vain.

The *U-19* has used up four of the five torpedoes she carries already and so, Krieger and his men have just one more mark to find before they can head home. He hopes it comes soon. They have been at sea for three weeks already and they are running low on food, their beards have grown and their hair is greasy because water is too precious to waste on washing.

Krieger puts the binoculars to his eyes once more and does another slow sweep of the horizon behind and then in front. Sea mist has formed in the mid distance and he lingers on the grey shadow of the low cloud. There's a shape forming out of the billows, it's too distant to make out clearly from here but significant as he sees the front profile.

The captain knows from experience what kind of vessel this is. His pulse races as he notices the three funnels, the tall mast, and the sharp point of the bow—even at this distance he can tell that it is some sort of destroyer. Krieger does not move straight away; he must gather as much information as he can about her while he is on the surface. He takes a sharp breath as he feels the excitement, for this is a real prize. It's nothing like those merchant ships with their doughy bellied sailors. This is a British destroyer, it will have a full complement of perhaps eighty sailors, there will be twelve-pound guns also and perhaps torpedo tubes. Krieger grins. He is about to take the binoculars from his eyes when he spots something else just behind the ship in the distance—it's easily as large, and holding pace with the first ship, is another tribal-class destroyer built for the British navy. This complicates things. Krieger must move fast, for if he can see these ships, then they most certainly can see him. He lowers the binoculars and stamps on the metal hatch below his feet, it takes a moment and it opens outwards for him to clamber down.

"Crash dive," he bellows into the darkness and is quickly inside, turning the wheel to lock the hatch up so that it is airtight. "North by northwest," he calls as he climbs down the ladder. "Destroyers, two of them. Dive!" A man with a patchy beard in a vest nods at him as Krieger takes off the heavy coat. "Red alert. All hands look alive. Switch to battery power."

The *SM U-19* judders as the ballast tanks fore and aft begin to flood with sea water. Two men turn the big valve handwheels and watch the depth gauge as they do. The front of the *U-19* dips down and they begin to dive properly. Nero's paws clack on the metal floor as she runs down the length of the U-boat towards the berth before the torpedo tubes, she jumps up onto the first bed to get out of the way. From experience, she knows when the boat dives the men are frantic. The diesel engine to the aft cuts out and the electric motor takes over, the bright white electric lights above the bulkheads dim to signal that they are going under the water.

Krieger climbs up a smaller ladder, here is the periscope with a chair next to the eyepiece. He sits down and grabs the handles to bring his face in. They will not be at periscope depth for another minute at least. Possibilities run through Krieger's mind—there are two destroyers and he has only one torpedo left. Two vessels represent double the danger to the

U-19 for once he fires, he will give his position away. His brow creases as he weighs up what to do. As long as they have not spotted them, he will be able to take out one at least. He is just about to give the order to load the fore torpedo tube when there's a huge boom from above his head. The *U-19* rocks right over to the port side from the blast. The men holding the ballast tank wheels fall against them. Charts and the compass slide from the control room bench. Nero's ears go flat to her head in worry as she huddles beside a pillow on the bunk. Spanners fall onto the floor in the aft engine room with musical clanks. The *U-19* rights herself by rocking the other way and there's another boom from above. Cold, salty seawater sprays in through gaps in the metal work above.

"They're shelling us," calls Krieger from beside the periscope. These two destroyers have spotted them already. "Keep to your stations," he calls out, "dive.' The two men at the ballast wheels regain their positions. Felix down in the engine room has been thrown to the floor between the two rows of machinery that drive the propellor. Stolz, the first mate, is positioned below the hatch to the world above, he fell against a bulkhead in the blast and is just recovering; his round glasses are at an angle on his face.

"Brace yourselves," he yells down the length of the U-boat. There's another boom, weaker than the first but still strong. The hammocks in the crew section swing violently. A bunch of hung up onions comes free and splits as it hits the floor. Felix manages to get to his feet. Three of the torpedo men at the front clasp hold of the last of their missiles to stop it rolling around and blowing up.

"East by fifteen degrees, hard turn," calls Krieger as he slips off the chair from the periscope and begins down the little ladder to the control room. One or both of the ships above will be shelling them, the deeper they dive the less impact any explosion from the artillery will have. If the *U-19* turns as well, they will also minimize the chance of being hit.

The U-boat continues the descent with the bow dipping downwards as they go deeper under the sea. A loose onion rolls down the space between the bunks towards the torpedo room. Felix gets to his feet between the rows of hammering, hissing machines and the blonde first mate straightens his glasses as he tries to stand up. There's another boom, but the *U-19* only rattles at this because the shell is far above them on the water. They are not out of danger. Krieger approaches the men at the ballast tank wheels and his eyes are fixed on the depth gauge—it is hovering at forty metres. He flicks the glass with his middle finger and it begins to fall again. The furthest the dial measures is sixty, they are getting close to fifty.

"Fifty-five metres and level her out," says Krieger. His voice is calmer now the explosions are further away. There's another boom from above, but it is more distant. They will have lost track of her. Krieger lets out a sigh.

In another few minutes, the *U-19* reaches the depth specified by the captain and the aft ballast tank fills with water to bring her down and level. Krieger orders the engine to half speed. They are fifty-five metres under—well out of harm's way. Sea water still runs through cracks here and there, and the *U-19* rumbles along under battery power with the structure creaking at the pressure from the sea outside.

Stolz, the first mate, presents himself to the captain. He has a small gash on his forehead. The man is tall for a U-boat sailor, he has short blonde hair with a flick and a parting, round glasses, and a piggy nose.

"What did you see?" he asks.

"Two destroyers, together." Stolz looks too thin to be in the Kaiserliche Marine, like he ought to be a schoolteacher or a church deacon.

"That's not usual."

"I know. It's possible there'll be another ship with them, someone they're protecting."

"Agreed," says Stolz. "Our course of action, Captain?" It's

rude for Stolz to say this. He should wait for orders rather than ask for them.

"Wait it out. We don't have the firepower for both ships and there may be more than just the two vessels." The blonde first officer nods even though his mouth wears a half-arsed snarl.

"Aye, Captain."

They have been at depth for an hour. Krieger filled in the logbook with the last coordinates and the exact time they went under. They have two hours maximum before they must resurface and have been going along at half speed under the water to keep the pistons moving. The *U-19* is beginning to get as cold as the water around them, and Krieger does not want to turn the heaters on because it will drain power from the battery and mean they have to surface more quickly. Under the water here, they are at least safe from enemy shells.

Krieger stands in the engine room in front of their chief engineer, a fellow called Felix. He's wearing a thick white jumper with braces and doesn't look like he's old enough to shave. At just over five foot two; he has patchy black wisps of beard growing from his chin and top lip. Felix has been busy with his men. After the near misses of the shells, he checked the hull integrity from within, there's a crack along the starboard stern above one of the diesel engines; Felix has tried to patch it up by welding a sheet of metal atop the crack. It's the best he can do in such circumstances. They have had trouble with the engines as well, if they get too cold, they sometimes won't start up again.

"You can't bring your dog on the next trip," says Krieger. It's an odd way to start the conversation.

"Why not?" asks Felix.

"What if something happens to her?"

"If it happens to her, then it happens to us."

"You know what I mean, Felix. She could get crushed or

stood on." The dark haired man gives a knowing grin.

"You've fallen for her," he says. Krieger nods in agreement. The crew have all fallen in love with little Nero; they have their black and white photographs and letters from home but the dog represents the only thing not specifically made to fight or support those that do.

"I want my bunk back as well," says the captain. Felix smiles. It's conversations like these that keep them human out here under the water where they might be drown or frozen or blown up at any minute.

"It's not good to be at this depth for long," says Felix. Krieger knows this already. They have pushed the U-19 to the edge of her capacity as a machine. "I think we've sealed the crack but I don't like the look of the battery, Captain. It needs ventilation—we need air."

"Do what you need to do, I won't keep us down here longer than is necessary." Felix nods as the captain steps through the round bulkhead door to the control room. He will need to keep an eye on the electrical batteries, they have to be regularly topped up with distilled water and ventilated to avoid the buildup of hydrogen gas which is poisonous. There's the air compressor as well—if this isn't working, they won't be able to fill the ballast tanks with air, and they won't be able to draw breath either, it all needs the air to work.

It's like they're up in space in many ways.

The longer they stay at this depth, the worse it is for the U-19 in terms of pressure on the hull and strain on the instruments and equipment. There's the constant dribble of seawater from splits in the steelwork, and the stink of salt, diesel, sweat and grease. The condensation from their breath runs off the outer walls, and water begins to pool at their feet in the control room so Krieger has his men switch on the bilge pump which will further deplete the battery. Nero has made her way back to the control room. She doesn't like the water on her feet, so one of the wheelmen has taken her on his knee. Her eyes are mournful as she shivers and looks back up at first mate Stolz leaning on the bulkhead.

Krieger checks his watch. Enough time has lapsed for the destroyers to have passed over, he hopes.

"All slow," he calls, and a sailor turns the telegraph wheel that signals to Felix in the engine room. It takes thirty seconds for the machine to respond. "Bring her up to periscope depth," he says. The men flood the ballast tanks fore, aft and at the port and starboard sides with air to make the *U-19* rise, it's a slow process if they want to keep the vessel level.

Again, Krieger climbs the little ladder to the periscope, sits down in the chair, grabs the handles, and pulls his face to the two eyepieces. With this, he will be able to look around without giving their position away.

"Periscope level, Captain," calls a voice from the control room. Krieger rotates the handle on the little wheel next to the machine to extend the tube above the waves. It takes a few moments for it to rise, and then Krieger can get a good look at the ocean above. Through the eyepiece, he does a mid-slow three hundred and sixty degree rotation and sees nothing but choppy grey water before a flat horizon. He knows from experience that he'll have to look twice; boats can get lost behind waves when your eyeline is this low. There's no sense of relief yet, the vessels he saw earlier could still be up there. At the last pass of the rotation, Krieger spots it some half a mile off the stern, the grey of a destroyer in the mid distance. He spends a few seconds concentrating on the shape and the smoke coming off the stack—the vessel is moving away from them. The destroyer will not be able to spot the periscope at this distance but it will see them if they surface. The sky above is a dark, angry grey and it's already raining. This is all good for the *U-19*. He calls down to the control room below.

"Dive. Ten metres. Half speed. South-southwest." He steps down the ladder and Stolz stands there waiting for him with his thin face dark and composed. He is not happy. The *U-19* rattles as the ballast tanks fill with sea water to bring them down. Felix the engineer enters from aft:

"We need to surface," he says. "If the diesel engines get any colder, they'll not start. The compressors need air as well."

"Give me ten minutes at full speed and we'll come up, the British Destroyer is heading away from us, possibly they have split up to search. Can you give me that, Felix?" The little man with the patchy beard nods and then goes back down to the engine room.

It does not take much depth to put pressure on the hull. They have been under too long. There are creaks from rivets. The dials on the gauges mist up. Bubbles natter in the ballast tanks. Water begins to gather on the control room floor. More of the salty North Sea sprays in from the leaks above and around them. These are undersea boats after all, they are not meant to be beneath the water this long. Krieger gets hold of Nero and walks her down to his bunk past the crew quarters near the torpedo room, he wraps her in a towel and puts her under a blanket. She looks up at him while she shakes. It could be fear or cold. Nero is not built for life on a U-boat, perhaps none of them are.

On his way back to the control room, Krieger passes the crew with blankets around their shoulders. Some sit on their bunks. Two swing from hooks on the ceiling in hammocks. It is claustrophobic even though it is freezing. Their eyes are round and their skin is pale from not seeing the sun enough. It has only been three weeks, but the lads are skinny, insipid reflections of the men they were on shore. One of them keeps coughing. Krieger nods and tips his cap as he passes. These men need to go home to Wilhelmshaven.

In the control room, the bilge pump is beginning to fail. Something might have got stuck in the pipe outside and the water on the floor is above the toes of his boots. Krieger reads the depth gauge as he passes, they are still ten metres below the surface. It has been twenty minutes, any longer and the *U-19* will crumple like a paper bag, even though they are not that deep. He will have to gamble on this one. It is something that Krieger does not like to do. This is the weight of responsibility.

Next to him, and looking down through his round glasses, Stolz focuses his blue eyes in silent and dumb defiance. The first mate here would have taken on the two destroyers at the drop of a hat, and then the *U-19* would be sunk at the bottom of the cold sea. It is Krieger's job to fight the war and also to bring the men and the U-boat back safely. He shall remind the tall, blonde man of this when they speak privately.

"Periscope depth," he calls, and the men holding the ballast control wheels begin to turn them.

"I am certain we'll have outrun them now, Captain," says Stolz. Krieger holds him with his brown eyes in silence. It's the kind of opinionated, dimwit rubbish he would expect from a merchant seaman who has more ambition than balls. Krieger is not going to cheapen himself or his men by taking this man on here. As he hears the tanks filling, he climbs the ladder to the periscope, his hand goes to turn the little wheel and he draws his face to the eyepiece. The *U-19* begins to rattle in strong currents and with the waves above. They are moving upwards slowly. In two minutes, Krieger can see the sky outside.

There's a storm. The sky is grey with rain and the waves are high. This is good. Krieger does a three hundred and sixty degree sweep with the periscope, slow and level. His eyes sting as he looks through the lenses. The air quality is getting worse and perhaps the electric battery is already leaking chlorine gas. Krieger cannot afford to get this wrong, for if they surface and there is an allied ship, they will face a pounding. Felix has warned him that the diesel engines may not start up because it's too cold, and so they will be a sitting duck. He makes another slow sweep with the periscope. There is nothing on the horizon but waves and rain.

"Surface," he calls down to the control room. He can hear the tanks filling with air and feel the front of the *U-19* rising as they move upwards. The waves begin to rock them from side to side as they go. Krieger climbs down the ladder and nods to Stolz.

"We're all clear," he says, "but there's a storm raging up there." Stolz gives him a wry smile back.

"It's not like the sea can sink us, Captain." The skipper does a sarcastic smile, as if the man has just told him the sky is blue. Krieger is less worried about what Stolz thinks than the other crew on the *U-19*. He raises his voice:

"Once we've got everything working as it should, let's make for home. God knows we've been at sea long enough, and we've done the best work we can. Is that five in the tally so far, lads?" He knows that it is. The two men who work the ballast hand wheels smile back at him, and as they do, Krieger sees warmth in their eyes.

"It's five alright," shouts one of the men on the other side of the control room. Krieger moves aft so that the crew can hear him:

"There's a drink waiting for all you lads when we get back to Wilhelmshaven," he bellows. "We're going home." Stolz turns his face to his captain and nods with a wide grin.

For once, the two men agree with each other.

CHAPTER NINE

The big brass bell of the *Kestrel* clangs in the first light of the freezing dawn. There's a brooding sky and an orange blaze shimmering over the water from the horizon. Skipper Williams has got a feeling. They're going to shoot the trawl.

It doesn't take long for Young Jack on the winch to haul the net from the deck and move it out over the ocean. He lowers the trawl doors into the choppy water first, these will keep the net open as it rolls along the seabed. The net follows and Woods keeps a careful eye on the cables and ropes to make sure they don't get tangled up; twice he has to call to Jack to stop the winch so he can lean over and straighten them out. The big iron machine squeaks as it turns, and the cables disappear into the slippery, inky water next to the *Kestrel* while she rocks on the waves. It takes about ten minutes.

The deckhands stand and watch. Big Billy claps his hands to keep them warm. George has found a black woolly hat in the bunk room. Cooper is having a cigarette through dirty fingers. The sky above is a dull, sickly grey with the *Kestrel* lonely in a flat landscape of nothing but sea on all sides. It makes George's legs go weak as he looks off the stern and at the emptiness behind them. There's the clunk of Woods as he approaches with his limp, he's managed to fix his wooden foot back in place. At the rails he lights up a cigarette and offers one to George. He shakes his head; he coughs enough as it is.

"What now?" asks George.

"We wait."

"How long?"

"That's up to the skipper, a couple of hours, maybe, while we drag it along the seabed. Then we haul the catch onboard and you'll start work proper. We'll shoot the net again and that's how it is till the fishroom is full." George nods. His breath makes steam in the cold air but it's better than the smell of grease, coal and men below deck. He looks out onto the lonely North Sea behind again.

"It must be a thousand miles back to Hull from here," says George.

"A thousand miles of nothing," answers Woods. His nose and cheeks are red from the cold as he blows out smoke.

Cooper and Big Billy are in the coal room. It's warm at least. On an old crate they are playing cards with Cooper sitting on an upturned bucket and Billy on a little stool. The game is called crown and anchor, and the boat rocks periodically to one side and then the next. Billy is unphased by the sea already.

"Do you ever take your cap off?" he asks Cooper.

"I'm ginger," he answers in explanation.

"So's my sister." Cooper looks up into his eyes.

"It's just the way I am. I keep myself to myself." Billy is not asking because he's rude. He just says what he wants. The coal stains on Cooper's hands are ingrained into every crease and fold of his skin, Billy's hands get like this too when he works the livery yard back in Etton. He examines the cards he's been dealt and plays a pair of threes; Cooper plays two queens.

"Where are you from?" asks Cooper.

"Etton." he doesn't know where this is. "Did you not fancy joining up?" He means volunteering for the war.

"I'm not fit to be a soldier," says Billy. "I don't do well with folk shouting at me. What about you?" Cooper keeps his eyes hidden under the lip of his filthy cap:

"I like to keep myself to myself. I do as I wish and I'll not be wearing a uniform. I don't like anyone coming near me, see." Billy plays three spades; Cooper plays a pair of threes. "Trawling suits me," he adds. Billy likes Cooper already because he's small and doesn't yap on too much. Periodically, the littler man will get up, open the hatch to the furnace and shovel in some coal from the heap around them. He has it all

89

in order. Billy feels calm with him there and will not mind losing the game to him.

Like all the folk on the *Kestrel*, Cooper is an oddball. He's not from Hull originally even if he sounds like he is these days. He knows how to hide. It's what he's good at. Cooper is from Aberdeen. He grew up on Walker Street in one of the big houses where families lived one to a room and he slept on the floor. Back then they called him Erica. His father and uncles were factory workers and drunks as well, and by the time he was thirteen, Cooper had been raped more times than he could count. It was normal even and, sitting at the one table they had with his grandmother, when his father and uncles were away at work, the old woman told him that it would have been much better and easier if young Cooper had just been born a man. He couldn't sleep that night for thinking about it.

The next day, early in the morning, he pinched a penny from his grandmother's purse. He stole his mother's two rings from under the floorboards, took his father's best flat cap, and was off into the world. Erica Cooper became Eric Cooper, and if he kept himself dirty enough and with that cap over his ginger hair, nobody would notice at all. Rotten teeth help as well. Nobody wants to get close enough, and since, Eric Cooper has worked trawlers from Newcastle to Grimsby, first as a deckhand and now as a trimmer. He is a quick and efficient worker, causes no trouble and would rather not be noticed by anyone. That's how it's stayed ever since. Cooper plays two jacks and his hand is finished.

"Let's play again," says Billy. Cooper must be careful with folk like Big Billy here, it's not that the tall man is a thug, far from it. Cooper feels the warmth from his uncomplicated nature, he liked him straight away and he must be watchful not to become too friendly. This is one of the ways Cooper has survived as he has for so long—there are no pals, he doesn't drink with the rest of the crew on the way home, he won't share the gossip either. With the war on, it is more important for him to stay out at sea, away from the cruel eyes of the world.

Peter Everett walks into the coal room. His head jiggles and his shoulders rock. He lifts the flap to look at the fire in the furnace, seems satisfied and then turns to the two men playing cards:

"The skipper will haul the net up in ten minutes," he says.

"How do you know?" asks Cooper.

"Intuition." Billy wrinkles his nose at the tall engineer as he stands there with his face wobbling and his head rocking.

"What happened to you?" asks Billy.

"Shell shock," says Cooper.

"What's that?"

"It means his nerves are all shafted, the engineer here was on board a big ship when she got torpedoed." Everett looks down on the two men playing cards. He does not like to be reminded. Billy is ready to understand rather than judge.

The hatch to the deck opens up and Jack taps down the ladder double speed. His face is bright and there's a big smile from ear to ear:

"The skipper's called it," he says. "We're hauling up the net." Seems like Peter Everett was wrong.

The real work begins. Now Big Billy realises why he's been fed so well and so often. It's not just because of the cold. The big, clunking winch has dragged the net up from the bottom of the sea and Billy watches as the headline breaks the surface.

Now the deckhands heave the rest of the loose folds of the net up by hand, Skipper Williams has the *Kestrel* sideways on to the waves. As the ship rolls backwards on the water, the line of four men heave. Big Billy is naturally good at this because of his strength. Once they've got most of the net on board, Young Jack winches it out of the water, and there it is, a huge, dripping ball of silvery fish in the cold morning air. John Grace barks orders from the open window of the bridge and they swing it onto the *Kestrel*. Woods goes to the cod end and unknots it so that the silvery catch spills out onto the deck, flapping and wriggling. It's mostly cod here but there are weeds, a spider crab, mud and rocks. Woods and Jack will check the net for holes, fix them up and then send it back down to the bottom of the ocean. Cooper spends a minute with the deckie learners Billy and George. With a knife in his coal stained fingers, he shows them how to gut, the innards go over the side, and he chucks the fish into one of the big buckets on deck.

In ten minutes, the deckhands are all on hand gutting; gulls fight and squawk in the wake, the wind is sharp and the deck is slippery with bits of fish and seawater. Woods tells a story about a ghost trawler out of Scarborough and he's got a good turn of phrase, it makes the time pass. Billy and George keep up the best they can against the skill of the other trawlerman, even Jack is an expert. The job is not so hard in itself, it takes a couple of hours to clean and gut all the fish, but then Jack explains that they will do the same thing every two or three hours, day and night, for the next seven days, and they do it all weathers too. Right now, the *Kestrel* rocks on the steady waves of the north water and though it's not always easy to keep your feet on the slippery deck, it's nothing compared to what the sea can become out here.

In the messroom they drink tea. The shifts have been worked out by the skipper. The new lads will take the first watch until the afternoon with Woods, and after dinner, they'll swap. John Grace, Jack, and Cooper will carry on in the darkness of the winter evening under the floodlights.

Just outside the sleeping quarters and round the corner, there's a tin metal bucket that the crew use for their business. As George Jackson takes a piss, he feels the ship dip down and then crest up over a wave he cannot see. The cold has got into him and the skin on his face feels raw from the wind. One of his coughing episodes is creeping upon him, and he readies himself for it. He puts his hand on the bulkhead behind the bucket, and keeps his head down while he coughs, it hurts his chest and makes his legs spasm in pain as he hacks up a pat of phlegm that he spits into the bucket. With watery eyes he looks down and there's a thick line of blood in it. It's normal to flush the bucket out and chuck the contents overboard when you've done your business. George is happy to get rid of it.

In another hour, Skipper Williams has ordered the net up again, and it's Billy and George hauling the net over the side of the ship while Woods operates the winch. The net is swollen with slippery cod this time and they spill onto the deck flapping and wriggling in the grey of the afternoon. The wind whips up and the lads fall to gutting. George is slow to start with, Billy is good with a knife, and Woods looks like he can do it in his sleep.

By teatime at six o'clock, George can hardly feel his feet, his hands are frozen and he is exhausted. He, Big Billy, and Woods sit down next to each other in the messroom and eat fried fish that Stout has probably spat all over. There's a stack of white bread already thick with margarine on each slice. They are too tired to talk, already, and it's only been one shift. George feels like he's been aboard a steam trawler for most of his life. Woods begins to make a fish sandwich and Billy copies.

"It's better than home," says Woods.

"Maybe for you." This is George. He works in the lumber yard; the job is physical and cold in the winter but you soon get warmed up with the lifting and cutting. On the deck of a trawler, you stand still and gut for an hour or more at a time. It's exhausting.

"How much will we get paid?" asks Billy with his mouth full of fish sandwich as he chews.

"Depends on the catch," answers Woods. "On a good one you might get five quid. The skipper reckons we'll get more because there's a war on and there aren't so many ships out fishing." Five quid is more money than Billy has ever had in his life. He momentarily stops chomping, then continues when he remembers that he's wanted for the murder of his own father. Five quid could get him a long way from Hull and Etton.

"What will you spend yours on?" asks George. Billy chews the last of his sandwich as he makes himself another.

"It'll be rent," says Woods with a sigh. "My mam and sister live off Tyne Street with my dad's cousin. If I get enough money, we'll move."

"Where's your dad?"

"At the bottom of the North Sea like my big brother." George is not used to this flippant way of speaking about the dead. Billy doesn't look like he's listening. The five quid would mean a lot to his mother back in Etton, he wonders how he could get it to her. The *Kestrel* suddenly lurches to one side, drops sharply and then banks back to the starboard, George leans on Billy in the movement and his stomach gurgles.

"How is this better than home?" he asks. Woods grins. He shouldn't explain, but these two are new to the *Kestrel* and in seafaring terms they are not even real people yet. Woods would never mention this to the other crew.

"My cousin's a proper big bastard. He took me and my mum and my sisters on when my dad died and he didn't do it in a glad way neither. He treats them like shite. If I was big enough, I'd put one on him." Woods manages to say this without sounding like it's genuine, even though it is.

"I'll hit him for you," says Big Billy. Woods doesn't register the comment and carries on:

"If I could work on the trawlers more, I'd be out all the time, and I'd be able to afford a place of my own for my mam and my sister. Then that fat bastard wouldn't be able to touch them." Now Woods has got started, the words tumble from his mouth in freshly formed ideas that he has not thought of before. "Maybe Skipper Williams will put in a good word for

94

me when we get back to port." Billy picks up his tin mug of tea and his throat bobs as he swallows the lot in two gulps.

"I'll batter him for you," repeats Billy as he wipes the tea away from his blonde whiskers with the back of his hand. Woods looks up to him.

"You serious?" he asks. Billy nods:

"Does he knock them about?" Woods swallows next to this giant of a man.

"Aye." It's actually worse than knocking them about. Mathews does other things that Woods won't admit.

"My old man used to belt my mother too, when he was pissed up," says Billy, "he picked on me and my sister. I put an end to it." He doesn't want to say much more. The offer is genuine, but Woods is not stupid, having Big Billy turn up at his front door and belt hell out of Mathews is a tempting daydream, but in reality, it would only make more trouble in the long run. Woods is glad of the offer though.

"You're a good one, Billy," he says. "You stick with me on this trip and I'll see you alright. You too, George." Woods realises that all he has to offer these lads is his knowledge of the sea and how to stay alive and safe on a trawler. Perhaps this is what Skipper Williams was asking him to do all along.

"Do you want that tea?" asks Billy. Woods shakes his head. Billy picks up the tin mug and finishes it in two gulps.

"It's six hours till we're next on deck, lads," says Tommy Woods, "we'll have to get some kip."

CHAPTER TEN

It's morning. The sea is never what you'd call calm, but there is a sense of peace after the storm. Krieger and the first mate, Stolz, stand on the bridge of the *U-19* with their binoculars to their eyes—the tall man has goggles over his glasses. The spray from the sea is cold.

Krieger has calculated that they're north of Scotland. They'll enter the North Sea, dive under the British blockade that stretches from Scarpa Flow to Norway and be home in Wilhelmshaven within the week. The mood of the men is much lifted in the last day since they shrugged off the two British destroyers. Felix is concerned with the diesel engines that power them now they are on the surface. There have been blockages to the coolant system—if they get too cold again, he is not sure if they'll fire up. There is something wrong with the pistons that drive the propellor also, perhaps a cracked cylinder too, it will all affect their mobility and it's a good job they are on the way home, but going under the British blockade will be a real struggle.

In the early morning, the *U-19* has come across something in the far distance that is of interest. Krieger has been summoned to the bridge on the conning tower to have a look at it with his experienced eyes and he scans the horizon till he finds the vessel in question. He can see through the binoculars that it's small and jolly already. There's a stubby funnel belching smoke into the sea air. It's a steamship, a trawler probably. Not worth a torpedo by any means. He scans the area in front and behind the vessel; it appears she is on her own. Krieger takes the binoculars from his face and turns to smile at Stolz beside him, the goggles give the man's face a pinched look.

"It's a fishing ship," he says. He calls down into the control room below: "Dive. Periscope depth!" They are going under.

Captain Krieger has done this more than a few times now.

He needs the light of the morning sun behind him as he surfaces, it will give the *U-19* a more commanding position, help them see better and scare the life out of the crew on board the trawler. The U-boat rattles as it moves under the water at periscope depth, there is definitely something awry in the way she judders. Krieger takes a look through the periscope and finds the ship off the starboard. On the deck he can make out little figures hauling up the nets along the side.

"What's she doing this far north?" asks Stolz from below. The first mate often speaks before he thinks.

"Catching fish, Stolz. That's what trawlers do." It's very unlikely this vessel will be armed, and the crew will be a pushover once the *U-19* swings the deck gun at them and threatens to shoot.

"More stupid fisherman. She's an easy target."

"So, she is. Everyone needs to eat, Stolz, that's no different just because there's a war on. We'll come up five hundred yards off the stern to give them a warning." He looks at his watch. "Ten minutes. Stolz, I'd like you to prepare your men to be on the deck, armed and ready." There's no need to waste a torpedo on this trawler. Krieger climbs down the little ladder from the periscope.

"Would it not be better to come in closer, Sir?" Krieger's brown eyes look up to the first mate and fix him with a stare. He should not be questioning orders, and Krieger does not need to explain them either. He ignores the comment.

"I want your men ready." Stolz swallows before moving off to the fore of the U-boat where the crew will be on their bunks. Krieger is also surprised that the boat is this far north, fishing is a much more dangerous business with a war on, as if it wasn't dangerous enough. He steps to the bottom of the ladder under the main hatch. Here he puts on his leather coat and fits his cap tight to his head. It will take the *U-19* ten minutes to come up behind the trawler. He will have to impress on Stolz the nature of this war when they speak in private. This modern conflict is not like anyone has fought before; they are not primitives who kill innocent men. The trawler will spot them as they rise off their stern, and the skipper will surrender as soon as he sees the conning tower. Krieger has a responsibility to the men of that fishing vessel as well as he does to the crew of the *U-19*.

"Begin the ascent," he calls to the sailors on the ballast tank wheels and the U-boat judders as the fore tank is pumped with air to lift the bow. The *U-19* is languid as it rises up from the ice-cold sea, and for one last time before they go back to Wilhelmshaven, Krieger and his men make ready to attack.

It's the morning shift.

They have been at it for forty eight hours solid, night and day. George now knows why Skipper Williams is sometimes known as the Old Fox, it is because he seems to know precisely where to dump the net and then when to draw it up out of the darkness. Almost every haul has been full and the tiny crew of the *Kestrel* have been worked to the bone. George's eyes are red from lack of sleep and his hands are stiff and raw, his chest has got progressively worse.

It's perhaps eight in the morning and Big Billy and George are hauling the belly of the net up on their own while Woods operates the winch. Skipper Williams is on the bridge with the window open looking down on the men at work on the deck of the *Kestrel*. Gulls natter in the wake. The wind is light but sharp from the west. The sun is just breaking the horizon behind and the sky is turning an icy blue. Here they are, in the middle of nowhere. For the last half an hour, under the direction of Williams from the wheelhouse, the three men have pulled the latest haul up from the seabed. They've nearly got it in.

It's Billy that sees the U-boat first. He doesn't lose his grip on the net when he spots the monster. The *U-19* cuts through the sea in the near distance behind as it rises up from the depths. Billy doesn't know what it is.

"Skipper!" he calls. "There's a ship behind us." Williams sticks his head out of the wheelhouse in the grey morning light and sees the sun coming up behind the U-boat. He blinks to make sure he's not seeing things. Williams did not really think they would meet an enemy vessel out here, as if the war is for other men fighting far away and not in these cold waters where he has spent his whole life. He considers the front profile of the long grey U-boat some five hundred yards away—he has just a few seconds to think about what they should do. He's good at making decisions.

Any other trawler skipper would ring the ship's bell and order the men onto deck. He'd cut the engines, haul in the rest of the net and then wait for the German vessel to move towards them. They'll not be shot, he's heard. At gun point the U-boat sailors will force the crew into the lifeboat, and then cast them adrift while they ransack the trawler. They'll be looking for anything they can nick as well as anything they can eat or get pissed on.

He rubs his leathery forefinger together with his thumb in thought. The *Kestrel* has a half full fishroom which will be worth a tidy penny back in Hull. They will be put out in not much more than a rowing boat at best, and they are probably six hundred miles off the south coast of Iceland. Williams calculates the chances of their survival—the shipping lanes are closed because of the war and the blockades, so they will most likely drift. Not only this, but Skipper Williams has a very expensive bottle of Swiss cognac in the cabinet next to his bunk. He brought it with him as a celebration of his last trip, and he does not at all want anyone else getting their hands, or lips on it. It takes the blink of an eye for him to consider all this.

There is only one course of action open to him. He goes back onto the bridge and puts his gnarled fingers onto the handle of the telegraph wheel, moves it to full ahead, and a little bell rings down in the engine room to relay the order. As soon as he's done this, he sticks his head out the window and bellows at Billy and George still hauling at the belly of the net:

"Get that bastard haul on board as quick as you can." This catch will help fill the fishroom. Skipper Williams is going to outrun this little German boat. He reaches out and takes hold of the rope hanging under the ship's bell and sounds out two sharp clangs into the morning. They will have to shoot him if they want him to stop. Young Jack appears at the bottom of the ladder to the bridge, he climbs up a few steps and sees the skipper through the open door.

"What is it?" he asks.

"All hands to get that net back on the ship, there's a U-boat behind us."

"A what?" Skipper Williams turns to look at the boy and his eyes are empty and cruel.

"You heard," he whispers. Jack did hear, but he didn't quite comprehend the words coming out of the old man's mouth. He steps back down onto the deck and looks out over the stern to the grey shape moving towards them. His blood runs cold for he can see dark figures on the deck and the outline of the twelve pound deck gun. Williams sticks his head out of the wheelhouse window to bellow at the boy:

"Stop gawking, you tit. I need that net hauling in so we can outrun her." Jack snaps out of it and moves off to help Big Billy tugging at the belly of the net. They are nearly there and, in a few moments, they'll see a line of white buoys break the surface. Cooper steps out of the messroom and adds his hands to the net as they haul. He looks up and sees the grey submarine giving chase in the mid-distance. His stomach churns. Below them, the *Kestrel* begins to creak as she speeds up. John Grace appears on deck and immediately looks over the stern, he too sees the *U-19* moving towards them in the cold morning with the sun coming up on the horizon behind.

"Bloody hell," he whispers under his breath. He steps into

the map room. John Grace is going for that rifle.

He knew they'd need it after all.

On the bridge of the *U-19*, Krieger steps in front of three of his sailors, and from under his peaked white cap with the Kaisermarine golden wreath badge on the front, he puts the binoculars to his eyes. He's already given the order for full ahead and for the bearing north by northeast.

"We should have come up nearer to them," says Stolz behind him. On other attacks they've surfaced right beside a fishing boat or a freighter, close enough to make the crew piss their pants. Stolz is definitely getting too big for his oversized shoes—Krieger will have to discipline him later. Through the binoculars, he can see figures on the deck frantically trying to haul the net back in. They will have seen the *U-19* already. If Krieger was within distance to call to them, he surely would. He turns to the two seamen next to him:

"Fire a volley of shots please gentlemen, over the bow, if you don't mind." The men shoulder their bolt-action Gewehr 98 rifles, and fire off a shot apiece, reload and then fire again. The gunshots ring out under the fresh, cold morning sky.

"They're trying to escape," says Stolz. He also has his binoculars to his eyes. He can see the big figure of Billy as he pulls at the net. Under the water on battery power, the *U-19* is slow, but here on the surface the twin diesel engines can get them up to sixteen knots on a good day. That will be fast enough to catch this frantic little trawler.

"I can see they're running," says Krieger. "It'll take us half an hour to catch them. I can't see there'll be many men aboard. We'll set them adrift, requisition whatever they've got and then sink it. We'll be on our way home within the hour." He says this loud enough so the men around him can hear. They are tired from this last three weeks at sea, where once there were clean shaven faces there are beards, their skin suffers from not seeing enough daylight, the fresh water has nearly run out and they are sick of the tinned food. There will be something to eat and drink on this trawler for sure. Krieger knows there'll be a bottle of something squirreled away onboard as well. It will take them a day to sail home and then, whatever brandy or whiskey it is, Krieger will stand on the deck in the winter sun and pass the bottle around his men in victory and happiness.

"We could fire the last torpedo and be done with it, Sir," this is Stolz again. He is ambitious and it makes him foolish. The tall blonde man looks down on Krieger through his round black glasses.

"Why waste it? These fishing lads don't have the stomach for a fight. They deserve a chance as well, just like anyone does."

"Better for us to get the job done and be on our way, Captain." Krieger takes the binoculars down from his face and turns to the taller man.

"You have much to learn, Officer. I could easily take your comments as subordination but since we're near the end of our journey I will not." Krieger will have to put this man in his place, at least out here not all the crew will hear it. "Those men are non-combatants, Stolz, we're soldiers, not murderers and, if we sink that ship without going through the pantry, we might miss what little treats they have stowed away. A soldier has to think first before he acts." The twin engines of the *U-19* are at full speed already and on the surface here, the vessel cuts through the water towards the trawler. Stolz bows his head to his captain in deference even though his little eyes under the glasses tell a different story.

Krieger looks through his binoculars once more. He can see that the trawler has now hoisted their catch out of the water in a big ball swinging from the gallows at the side of the boat. They will be bringing the catch in, hoping they can make a run for it. Krieger is sad for them, genuinely, because they will never outrun the *U-19* and he will have to sink their trawler and then cast them adrift. He doesn't blame their captain for running, he's probably terrified, but it would be much easier for all concerned if they just gave up.

"Another two rounds each, please gentlemen. I'd like you to hit the boat so they know we mean business, but like I explained to your first mate here, we're not murderers." The sailors shoulder their rifles but this time they squint into the telescopic sights above the bolt-action. They fire a shot each and their shoulders recoil, they reset the bolt and repeat.

The gunshots sound eerie in the silence.

In the wheelhouse of the *Kestrel*, John Grace has the rifle in his hands. His nostrils are flared as he looks across to the skipper with the wheel in his gnarled fingers. There were many thoughts that crossed the Scouser's mind when he saw the U-boat in the distance, first that they would lose the trawler and the catch, next that he would still be in debt back in Hull, and then finally, that he might not ever get back at all.

"What are you doing?" he growls at the skipper.

"We'll bring the net onboard and we'll outrun it." John Grace would like this to be possible but he's a man of reason, unless he's sitting at a card table with a belly full of ale.

"We can't outrun that, it's a bloody U-boat. It's a military vessel." Skipper Williams takes his eyes off the sea in front.

"You'll do as you're told, Grace," he hisses. "What do you think we should do, turn round and wait for them to catch up?" This is rhetorical.

"Yes. There are rules. They'll put us adrift." Williams scoffs at this, and his lips curl in a snarl:

"We'll be dead just the same if they do. It'll be hundreds of miles to land. You know that. What bloody chance do you think you'd have in a rowboat in winter?"

"If we run it will make it worse."

"You're afraid, Grace. That's it. You think if we play by the rules, it will all be fine. That's why at your age you're still a first mate." Grace's brow furrows as he darkens.

"You're too old for this, Skipper, you should be at home in your pipe and slippers." Williams smiles to reveal his blackened teeth. He likes the fight, he always did.

"I'm still the Skipper, Grace. We run, and if they catch up to us, we keep them off as best we can. How many bullets have we got for that rifle?"

"You're not serious… There'll be more than twenty armed men aboard that U-boat. If we fire one shot back at them, they'll have every right to sink us where we sail."

"They're going to do that anyway. They've already shot at us, or did you not hear?"

"Warning shots, Skipper. If we don't turn this trawler around, we're dead men." Williams is calm momentarily, and his old face turns back to the sea in front.

"We're dead men if we do, Grace."

The German sailor holding the Gewehr 98 rifle is called Muller. He is good with it. As a young man his father showed him how to shoot pigeons and rabbits in the forest south of Rostock. There was a travelling fair that came in early October when the nights started to draw in, and there was always a shooting gallery where you could aim at wooden targets and stuffed colourful birds.

Muller knows how the waves feel beneath his feet, he can smell the salt air through his thick, dark moustache. He narrows his eyes over the four hundred or so yards to the deck of the trawler, and dangling outside the bridge is the ship's brass bell. The captain told him to hit the boat and Muller thinks back to the dark nights with his father standing beside him as he took aim in that shooting gallery all those years ago. He aims above the target and breathes out slowly as he squeezes the trigger and the rifle recoils. The bullet flies in a low arch over the freezing, choppy waters of the North Sea. Deep below there are pale fish and white spider crabs on the ocean floor in the darkness, above the *Kestrel*, gulls complain and squawk against an ice blue sky and the spray from the freezing waves. The bullet hits the bell of the *Kestrel* with a clang, like Muller is winning a prize at the travelling fair. It ricochets into the wheelhouse through the open door, whizzing past John Grace's ear and in front of Skipper William's nasty eyes fixed on the ocean in front. It thuds into the toughened glass of the window on the opposite side but does not have enough power to go all the way through. There it stays, embedded in the glass.

The two trawler men look at each other.

The skipper is right. They will have to run.

Grace leans over to the open door and yells at the top of his voice:

"Clear the bloody deck!"

CHAPTER ELEVEN

In the engine room, Cooper and George have opened the boiler furnace hatch and are shovelling in as much coal as they dare. Cooper does not remove the flat cap as he works. George breaks a sweat. They go quickly, and not just because they are under orders from the skipper—their lives are at stake. Williams has told them to fill the furnace to get it hot, and then bring Peter Everett to meet them in the messroom as soon as they've finished.

"It's a German U-boat," says Cooper as he loads another shovelful of coal with a scrape. Peter Everett stands at the side of the boiler with a kind of smirk, he knows that these rough working class trawlermen commonly take the piss. He thinks this is what they might be doing.

"You're talking shite," he says. Peter Everett does not swear. It was a U-boat that sent the *HMS Pathfinder* to the bottom of the sea and nearly drowned him. It's a U-boat that has made him shake the way he does and why his wife does not want him in the house, and why he has been discharged from the navy.

"It's true," says George. "A long grey thing behind us."

"Skipper wants us all in the messroom after we've filled the furnace." Cooper peers into the red hot of the fire and closes the grate. "She's full up for now," he says. Peter Everett's eyes are wide and his nostrils are flared.

"I have to see it for myself," he mutters.

"We're off to the messroom," says Cooper.

"I'll be right behind you two."

Peter Everett shivers at the bottom of the little ladder that leads up to the deck. His teeth chatter like he's cold. His hands can hardly grip the steel sides as he climbs up.

In the bright cold of the deck outside, he keeps low to the slippery floor and moves to the starboard rail to look out behind. His chest rattles as he shakes, but he cannot stop himself. He has to see this U-boat that is gaining on them under the grey sky above. Peter Everett's long fingers clasp the rail and he lifts his head up to look over the stern of the trawler through the gulls that still natter at each other. Everett's teeth chatter yet. He is panting. His stomach churns as his eyes search the horizon.

There it is. A grey shape cutting through the waters behind them some four hundred yards away, the conning tower is proud above the waves. Peter Everett takes a deep breath right into his chest as he steadies himself. This is the nightmare that has plagued him. Like the shell shock crept up when those fishermen dragged him onto their boat from the sea, so now, it leaves him. The fear is real, he can see it, and the worry is not hiding in his nightmares waiting to strike when he does not expect. It is right here. Perversely, he feels calm.

Everett creeps back down towards the messroom and, crouched behind the bulkhead, he looks at his long hands as he holds them up to his face. For the first time, he is not shaking. It's like magic, as if the real fear has washed the shaking away.

Peter Everett enters the messroom and the whole crew are there. Stout leans on the door to the kitchen. Cooper and Grace stand against the far bulkhead. Big Billy and George sit next to Woods on the bench by the table. Young Jack has hold of the ship in the wheelhouse above. He'll be shitting it. In the centre of the room is the stooped figure of Skipper Williams.

"You just powdering your nose, were you?" he asks Everett. The engineer stares back at him and for the first time in many months, he is not shaking like a leaf in the wind.

"They'll catch us up," he says. Everyone in the room knows what he's talking about.

"You'll have to make her go faster, then," says Williams.

"She won't."

107

"She'll have to."

"We're going to die," says Everett but not in a frantic way, more as a matter of clear and simple fact. He is not a trawlerman. He's lived a life on boats, aye, but not like this one. There have been rules and clear orders, fixed uniforms, and positions with regulated shifts. It's fear that has stopped Peter Everett from shaking. Skipper Williams sighs as he looks at this thin and earnest man who is nothing at all like the rest of the crew. Everett does not really understand the fatalism that these northern fishermen share. "Do you understand?" continues the engineer. "As soon as they get close enough, they'll riddle this nasty little tin can with bullets." Peter Everett does not raise his voice as he says this.

"You can piss your pants all you like, son." Skipper Williams uses sarcasm, not as a weapon, more as a tool to move the conversation forward. "I want you in the engine room, you can polish the little handles and oil the pistons but do whatever you can to make that engine go faster." Peter Everett licks his lips.

"It won't go any faster. That's what I'm trying to explain." Skipper Williams is not going to fall apart in this situation. There have been storms, sinking ships, injured, and dying men onboard, blood, guts, and shite all over the decks before, this is no different. Williams continues with the orders:

"Stout'll carry on as normal, these boys will still need to be fed whatever happens. Is there any of you lads know how to shoot a rifle? I don't mean one of them gat guns at Hull Fair, I mean like the one Grace has in his hands here?" The crew look over to John Grace standing with the long rifle.

"I can shoot it," says Big Billy. He really can, as a younger lad he helped the gamekeeper back in Etton. Skipper Williams fixes him with his cold eyes and Big Billy looks down through his blonde hair. He's always had a problem with orders has Billy, but there's something different about this miserable old man. Williams is not going to ask how Billy knows. He's just going to trust that the man is not lying, his instincts tell him that he isn't.

"Get to the stern, that's the back of the boat. Keep down. You can see what they're up to through the sights on the rifle, but don't shoot unless you have to." Williams beckons at Grace to give him the rifle. The Scouser seems reluctant and so the old man walks a few steps and takes it from him. The skipper turns to the rest of the men gathered; he must appraise them of what he's thinking:

"If they catch up with us, then the best that can happen is they put us onto the lifeboat then sink the ship. If they do that, then the chance of us getting to shore is low to bloody zero." He considers the men around him in the little messroom with their pale, frightened faces.

Outside it is deathly cold. There is a full net of fish on the deck they dare not gut. The sky is turning angry black in the late morning and behind the *Kestrel* is a German U-boat, the weapon that has already changed the nature of war at sea.

"We'll not outrun it," says Peter Everett again. Now he's not shaking he looks like a different person.

"We'll bloody try," answers the skipper.

The engine room towards the stern of the *U-19* smells of diesel and there's banging from the pistons along each side. Felix has oily fingers and his shirt is open to his chest in the heat. This is the only part of the vessel that is warm. He is showing the captain the problem with the engine, and the two of them are alone in the narrow space between the machines. Normally Felix's little dog, Nero, sits in a basket under the big petrol tank. The dog will probably be down in the bunk room with the other men.

"I think one of the cylinders is cracked," Felix has to raise his voice a little to be heard.

"How do you know?" asks the captain.

"I can hear it, the acceleration isn't as good as it was,

109

neither is our speed." Krieger listens to the rat-ta-ta of the engine for a moment—it sounds the same as always to him, but Felix here is one of those mechanics who almost senses what is wrong with a machine. He has a stethoscope he uses to listen to the engine but this time round he just knows what's wrong.

"Is this the fastest we can go?"

"In a straight line, yes." It's not meant to be sarcastic. Felix has blue, earnest eyes. He's not the kind to kid you around. "We've been hammering her for the last few thousand miles, Captain. Long periods of extreme pressure will crack a cylinder head, no bother."

"Can you fix it while we're moving?"

"I can't get near it until we've stopped dead." Felix, like the whole of the crew on the *U-19*, knows that they are chasing a trawler north and that their pursuit has been more than an hour so far and they have not got near enough to yell at the other men on board. The *U-19* is going too slowly. The engine is packing up. Young Felix should not say what he is about to, but he is tired of being trapped in a U-boat. He's been here for three weeks; he stands in the same stinky clothes; he is hungry for fresh food, dry land, and the big, warm whorehouse in Wilhelmshaven.

"Can't we just leave that fishing boat, Captain? Can't we just leave her and turn round? It's not like she's part of the war anyway." Felix is only saying what all the men, including Krieger, are thinking. The captain shakes his head. Felix continues. "The rest of the crew have had enough; I've had enough as well and so has this engine. So has Nero."

"I am sorry, Felix. Now we have seen her and she has seen us, we'll have to finish her off. Those are our orders." Krieger's voice can just be heard above the hammering noise of the pistons around them, and his eyes are gentle. A good sailor is careful and methodical, jobs on a ship must be done properly and with intention because it is this machine on which all lives depend. Krieger applies this attitude to soldiering too—he must complete the job. He doesn't really need to explain to Felix, but he will anyway:

"If every German ship does not do her duty, even in the face of odds that are not favourable, then we will have failed our Kaiser and our country. Do you understand, Felix?"

"We left those two destroyers."

"To preserve our lives and the *U-19*."

"But it's a fishing boat," he whispers back, not in subordination at all.

"It doesn't matter what kind of vessel it is. We've seen it. We will give chase and we'll send it to the bottom of the ocean as we have been tasked to do. Do you understand that? A soldier is nothing without orders and duty, just as a man is nothing without the will and guidance of God. Do you see, Felix? It is in these tasks that we are tested. We will not back down because to do so would break the code of who we are. Do you understand?" Felix nods. He does. He knows this dogged determination and resilience. It's how he knows the Kaiser will win this war.

"I'll check everything while we're moving. It might be a piston ring that has come loose, it might not be that bad. I'll do my best, but I don't think I'll be able to get more than sixty percent out of the engine, not without stopping."

"Keep on with it, Felix, you've always done the best you can, and I thank you for that. We'll give it another hour; we'll have caught up to her by then." The engineer smiles up at Krieger. They are friends.

"Thank you, Captain," he says.

Cooper and Young Jack have come through into the engine room and there is Peter Everett with a rag in his hand, his shirt open and the sleeves rolled up. He's just tightened one of the pipes with a big spanner and his arms look long and gangly. The white electric light flickers on the roof under a grate, and there's the noise of clunking as the engine works. The skipper has told Everett to get the *Kestrel* moving more quickly. He's doing his best.

He takes a long screwdriver from the floor and holds the blade onto one of the cylinders, leans down and then gently puts the handle to his ear. He couldn't do this if he was still shaking.

"What are you doing?" asks Jack.

"Listening to her." He means the engine. On the *HMS Pathfinder* they had a stethoscope for this kind of thing. Peter Everett blinks as he hears the purring from the machine. "It seems okay to me."

"Can't you just whack her on the arse like she's a horse?" says Cooper. Everett looks across at the grubby trimmer. He doesn't have the ready and easy language that these trawlermen do. He's used to the officer's mess where they are straight and polite.

"Can't we just chuck more coal onto the fire to get it hotter?" This is Young Jack with his bowl haircut and big, rabbit front teeth.

"It doesn't work like that; more steam won't generate more power. The engine's running at full capacity already," explains Peter Everett as he takes the long screwdriver handle away from his ear. Jack looks up at the man who doesn't shake any more. The last engineer, that Bacon fellow, would just tell Jack to piss off if he asked any questions—like most people do. Cooper doesn't say anything, but he is learning as Peter Everett explains.

"There are a few things we could do to move faster, I could adjust the throttle valve, that would let more steam out and make the pistons move faster, but we run the risk of breaking them if we do that."

"What else?" asks Jack.

"Lose some of our weight."

"Every time we burn coal, we get lighter," says Cooper,

"but we still need a tonne of it to get back home." You can never see Cooper's eyes, but his tone doesn't sound hopeful.

"How come you're not shaking anymore?" asks Jack.

"I'm not sure," answers Everett, "but when I saw that U-boat behind us, I felt my legs go weak and my heart do a double beat in my chest." Everett swallows as he frowns down at the engine. He is trying to explain it to himself using the only analogy he can understand. "It was if I'd been running too fast and someone adjusted the throttle so I could go back to running at normal speed." He does not know if this is true.

"First Mate Grace says you got hit by a torpedo." This is Young Jack again with his eyes narrow under the flickering light of the engine room. He's mature enough to operate a trawl winch, use a gutting knife and he can fix a net as fast as anyone, but the social skills have yet to develop.

"I was," he answers.

"What was it like?"

"I was on board the *HMS Pathfinder*. She was huge. It felt like thunder when we got hit, but I shouldn't worry, lad. If that U-boat decides to torpedo us, we won't even know about it." Jack swallows. Cooper puts his hands on both the lad's shoulders and turns him round.

"Let's leave him in peace, Jack," he says.

Big Billy is on deck in first mate Grace's sheepskin jacket. It's too small for him. Woods has given him his woollen hat, and he has a blanket over his shoulders. He's positioned himself behind the lifeboat, and the rifle Grace gave him rests across its bow pointing at the grey German U-boat following behind. Billy has been here for half an hour and the vessel has hardly gained on them in all this time. At various points, he's noticed movement on the bridge and thinks he can see men looking through binoculars at him but he can't be sure. Billy knows they will have seen him.

At first, he reasoned that the Germans would catch up to

113

them quickly, given how slow the trawler moves, but now it just seems like they're following behind. Grace says they're armed with torpedoes and might be lining up to fire one off. Skipper Williams thinks they'll come up alongside and board. Billy hasn't thought what he'll do if that happens, it was only a week or so past that he was running from the coppers after what he'd done to his old man. It's best not to worry about things, that's what his mother says, you get all bothered if you start to think too much. Billy struggles not to think as he looks out at the frozen sea behind him, he is used to the peace of the East Riding Wolds but out here, it is desolate with a pancake flat horizon. His breath makes steam in the cold air and he looks down the sights of the rifle at the U-boat some four hundred yards behind.

There's movement from next to him and crawling from around the messroom close to the bulkhead, is Woods. He comes up behind Billy and the big man looks down on him over his shoulder.

"I've brought you something," says Woods. Billy reaches out his hand from under the blanket and collects the tin cup. The fumes tell his nose it's hot and sweet. "There's brandy in that." Woods looks out to the U-boat in pursuit with wide eyes. "Has it got any closer?" he asks. Before Billy answers he puts the tin cup to his lips and sinks the lot in a gulp. Then:

"They're just following," he says. Woods collects the tin cup from him.

"Do you want another one?" Billy nods. Woods takes two minutes to return with another mug of tea, sugar, and brandy. Billy sinks this one a little slower than the last. His eyes moisten. Uncharacteristically Billy says:

"Thanks." Woods smiles.

"Do you want me to take over?" Billy shakes his head as he stares over the lifeboat to the sea behind. He likes to protect people; it feels natural. He'd rather be out here freezing half to death than in the messroom listening to Stout babble on.

"What do you think they're waiting for?" asks Woods.

"They're hoping we give up."

"What makes you think that?"

"I've seen a bloke on the bridge there, behind the rails twice now. He aimed a rifle at me, I think. If he's got a good enough sight, I reckon he'd hit me as well."

"So, they're watching us?"

"Aye." This information makes Woods feel nervous.

"Why aren't they shooting then?"

"I used to hunt deer out at Dalton Forest when I was a lad. You could never kill them dead in one shot, but if you clipped them sometimes, we'd just follow till they ran out of steam."

"Is that what they're doing to us?" He looks back to Woods with his big blue eyes that are moist from the tea and brandy. Billy doesn't answer the question.

"You know if we make it back to Hull, Woods, I'll come and batter your uncle for you, I'd enjoy it."

"Ok," he answers. Woods doesn't want him to do this.

"My dad used to batter my mam as well."

"You said."

"I fixed it in the end."

"What happened?"

"Probably doesn't matter now what I did, does it?" Woods has managed to wedge himself between the bulkhead and the lifeboat. His teeth are beginning to chatter in the freezing air.

"What did you do?"

"I killed him." Woods swallows. You hear all sorts from men, especially when they've had a drink, and especially in situations where they're afraid, it's more often than not shite, but he gets the feeling that Big Billy here is telling him the truth. "I had a fight with him outside a pub in Beverley. We'd both had a drink, only he's not as big as me. He was a dirty bastard and I know how he fights. I picked the right shot to clobber him in the chin and he went down backwards, so I left him. Turns out he smashed the back of his head when he hit

115

the cobbles." Billy has not really considered any of this and it is coming out of his mouth as fully formed ideas. "The coppers are looking for me." Woods screws up his face.

"And that's why you're here?"

"Aye."

"You're an animal, Big Billy. Thank God you're on our side." Billy gives a wide grin that shows the gap between his front teeth over his underbite. Woods has never seen him smile before. "Do you want another tea and brandy?"

"Go on then."

A body adapts quickly to a situation. George Jackson is in the tiny corner that passes for their toilet. He stands above the bucket, coughing. For the three minutes that he splutters, he forgets that he is six hundred miles north of Scotland midway between there and Iceland, probably. As the spasms rack his body with pain, he forgets too that there is a U-boat trailing the *Kestrel,* and that it will either sink them or put them adrift on a little lifeboat. When the coughing stops, he wipes his face with the handkerchief from his pocket and it is bloody. His condition is getting worse with the cold and the work. Perhaps he should have stayed at home and accepted that he was not made to go to war like his brother, Sam.

In the galley, Stout has brewed up tin mugs of sweet tea with brandy in. They would never do this, but the situation is exceptional. John Grace looks out of one of the round windows at the sea going past, the weather is getting worse outside. Behind him, George returns from the toilet and sits on the bench in front of his mug of tea. Upstairs in the wheelhouse, the skipper will be steering the boat through the rough seas. Grace is frightened of how cold the old man is up there. It's just him and George Jackson alone in the messroom.

"I bet you wish you'd never set foot on this trawler," says Grace without looking at the man.

"Wishing doesn't do you any good," he answers and is

116

pleased with this reply. Grace turns to him and examines the brown hair, sunken eyes, and white skin.

"You look like shite, son," he says. George really does. His skin is deathly pale and Grace mistakenly takes this for fear. He heard George coughing over the bucket and thought it was him being sick. He wants to help. "A better man than me said, if you worry, then you go through the pain of something twice." Grace can't remember where he heard this.

"Is that so?" says George. He is not usually rude.

"I'm trying to help."

"Thanks." This is sarcasm. "I think you're more scared than I am," says George. "You keep looking out the window, and you're pacing up and down just because the skipper said we can't go out on deck."

"That's because I know what's coming, son. As soon as it starts raining, the drops of water will freeze all over this ship. It happens all the time when you get this far north, and when it does, you and me and all the crew will have to take hammers and spanners and get out there to chip it all off, because if we don't, the bastard ship will keel over into the water with the weight. What do you think will happen while we're chipping? Them bloody Germans and that U-boat will start shooting us." Grace is red faced and his voice is getting louder. He does not like to be kept waiting, and if the Germans are set to finish him off, he would rather they just got on with it so that he and all the debts that weigh heavy on him can sink to the bottom of the cold sea forever. George Jackson regards the red faced Scouser with a pale stare.

"A good sailor can't be impatient," he says.

"What the hell do you know about sailing?"

"Nothing at all." It's not like George Jackson to smirk, but the situation is as ridiculous as it is bad. The dark humour of the trawlermen and the grey rolling rain clouds outside lend shadows to George. He is learning to take the piss, as he should.

CHAPTER TWELVE

The afternoon draws in and the sky that was grey before is turning inky black as the sun goes down. There's no rain thankfully. It is freezing outside but nothing has frozen up like John Grace said it would. The U-boat has been on the tail of the *Kestrel* for some two hours and she's getting further away.

Stout has cooked a stew and some of the crew are just about to sit down and eat. Skipper Williams, Jack, Woods, and Peter Everett who is still not shaking anymore, are all present at the table. Stout hands out dishes of the stew with fat bread rolls and the four men begin to eat. John Grace will be steering the ship up in the wheelhouse and Cooper has the engine room under control along with George to shovel coal if it's needed. It's as if there is nothing wrong at all and they are not being hunted into the ice sheets of the north by a dull-grey U-boat less than half a mile behind. The door to the messroom opens and Billy's tall figure stoops to step through. He has a blanket around his shoulders and his face looks red. In one of his big, raw hands is the rifle.

"It's gone, Skipper," says Billy. Williams looks up to the farm lad. He knows what he means but wants to be sure.

"What has?"

"That U-boat."

"What happened?"

"I must have fallen asleep, and when I opened my eyes, it was gone." Williams does not have time to wonder how a body can fall asleep on the freezing cold deck at this time of year. He gets to his feet and fits his cap over his white hair. At the door he unhooks his duffle coat and puts it on.

"You lads have your tea," he orders. "Me and Billy here'll go have a look." There's no sense of urgency to his voice. The two men make their way outside, into the darkening afternoon, and down the slippery decks to the stern where they stand next to the lifeboat and look at the wake from the propellors. The steam engine buzzes under them and there's a line from the back of the boat stretching out into the cold glassy water. The flat sea around them is a world of difference from the rolling waves of the storm a few days before, sure enough, there is nothing at all on the horizon with the sun setting off to the west. The U-boat has gone. Skipper Williams scans the distance with his binoculars.

"How do you fall asleep in this cold?" asks the old man. He's not angry. He doesn't take the binoculars from his eyes.

"I just do, if I'm bored enough." Williams is respectful to Big Billy. He is used to dealing with unruly men who have a sense of pride, they are often not unreasonable. He understands them because he was once so himself and full to the brim with anger and bile. After his uncle died, Williams learned to keep his hatred locked up in his chest, and to let it out bit by bit like the whistle on the steam engine stack behind him. It comes out in barbed comments and in his evil stare, but he likes this big, unpredictable man standing next to him in the dusk. Like the sea, Big Billy is not something you can control.

"I don't think they've gone," says Skipper Williams. He is confiding in this big man. Billy looks out into the sky that is a few minutes away from turning black.

"What do they want with us anyway? We're not soldiers."

"I don't know, but I wouldn't leave us alone, if I were their skipper, Billy. We catch fish that feeds the folk back home, and the Kaiser won't like that. Just like we've got a blockade to stop them getting out to the Atlantic so they can't feed themselves. Given half the chance I'd sink us just to stop us putting food on the table." Billy narrows his eyes at the horizon as he listens. He knows there's a war on, but the reasons for it are clouded in mystery—it's not Billy's business how governments use their money and armies.

"What are we going to do then, go home?" Williams lowers his binoculars so he can look up at Big Billy's smooth face.

119

"We can't go home yet; we haven't got a full fishroom."

"What about the U-boat?"

"We'll just have to pretend she's fucked off."

Big Billy likes Skipper Williams because he's a bastard. He's a bastard, and he's got a big pair of bollocks.

George didn't realise that trawlers fished at night. They have big electric lights on the front of the wheelhouse like two bright circular moons shining down on the deck. The night sky is oily black and the wind is not strong, but as cold as death.

This is the first of the new shift, Billy, Woods, and George are on deck and Cooper is down in the engine room. They will be six hours on and six hours off, like before. It will be as if the encounter with the U-boat didn't happen at all. They've gutted and stored the haul they brought in when the U-boat turned up, fixed the net and fired it off the side of the trawler into the black water, and the *Kestrel* powers ahead under Grace's watchful eye from the wheelhouse. The night is cold, and now they've got the first trawl over the side, they can get inside to warm themselves up.

"The engineer's gone back to shaking again," says Woods as they sit down in the messroom. "He reckons it's something wrong with his nervous system. He says it's had too much energy pumped through it, like when you crack one of the piston heads on an engine so it judders." George and Billy take their places next to him.

"I had a Jack Russell used to shiver like that when it was thundering outside," says Big Billy. Stout has left some of the stew from earlier that didn't get eaten, and they scoop it out of the saucepan with their tin cups.

"He's had the shit scared out of him," says George. "I can't say I wouldn't be the same." Billy slurps down his tin cup of stew and reaches the mug down into the pan for a refill.

George wonders what time it must be, it feels like the

middle of the night but it's probably only eight o'clock. His hands are tight from being in gloves and his feet sting inside his boots, he thinks about home. He knows that his mother will be more worried about what happens to Sam now that George isn't there to stop him getting into bother. He should really get back as soon as he can, there are things that will need sorting. Who'll have filled his mam's coal store at the back of the house, how will the lumber yard be without George to organize the order sheet? This trip is a distraction for him, and the danger has clarified his duties while this dark water has given him a sense of grim fatalism. He's needed in Cottingham, not in the middle of the North Sea.

"A day of this and we'll be full," says Woods. Billy takes a gulp on his stew and looks inside the tin cup now it's gone.

"Best food I've ever had," he says, and means it, "I don't care if that bastard cook spat in it." He means this as well.

For Billy, the *Kestrel* is a fine and welcoming place. There's food enough, always someone to talk too and plenty to keep you occupied. The cook is an arsehole, but he's no worse than the yard boss down at the farm. Billy's mother loves him, but she shouts and to save his earholes, he scoots off to the alehouse over in Etton and spends what little he has on ale because he's bored and they won't let him sit in there for free. If it's not the Light Dragoon at Etton, it's the Bay Horse in North Burton or he might walk all the way to Beverley. Wherever he goes there's always some tosser who mentions his size and says something that Big Billy can't pretend he didn't hear—so there's a fight. Billy wins and then he's in trouble. On the *Kestrel*, he's not bored and there's no drink, apart from the brandy Woods brought him earlier, that just made him sleep. Big Billy is not used to men like George and Woods here, not the Skipper neither, nor Cooper—they treat him as if he's useful, it's an odd feeling. Men don't have to know about your lives and they don't seem overly keen to explain about theirs. Billy doesn't mind the constant rise and

121

fall of the boat, or the cold, and as long as he's fed enough, he'd rather stay on the *Kestrel*. It feels like home.

"I'll be glad to get back to Cottingham," says George. "I've things to attend to there."

"Family?" asks Woods.

"My younger brother. He's a dickhead at the best of times. He signed up for the front. I don't know when he'll be going."

"How come you didn't sign up with him?"

"The doctor said I've got something wrong with my lungs." George already told him this. Woods takes a slurp on his stew from the tin cup. The electric light flickers. The *Kestrel* rocks to one side. Woods stares out the window of the messroom into the darkness before he speaks:

"I don't want to go home ever again," he says, "if I make enough money from this trip, I'll move my mam and my sister out my cousin's place on Tyne Street. We'll rent somewhere and I'll be the man of the house. We won't have to live under that bastard's roof anymore."

"Good luck with that," says George. It's not sarcastic. Woods sighs. He knows he's kidding himself:

"Maybe after five trips I'd have enough. I'll have to give him the best part of my wages for their rent and board while I've been gone."

"I've already told you," explains Billy, "I'll belt him."

"That'd make it worse. Once you'd kicked him up and down the street, me and my mam and my sister would still have to live there. I'll have to deal with him myself. I don't know what I'll do."

"How much would you need to get out of there?"

"God knows, twenty quid, maybe more." George blows out air. This is a lot more money than these men can hope to earn from this trip put together.

"Will we really get five quid when we get home?" asks Billy.

"It could even be more if the price of fish is high," says Woods. Billy reaches over and scrapes his tin cup along the bottom of the saucepan to get the last of the stew.

"What would you do with it?" asks Billy. "I mean with the five quid." In this short journey so far, Billy has not really considered that he would be paid for his efforts. Back home in Etton, part of his salary is that he and the family can live in their tiny cottage. There's money to feed themselves, but not well, and also enough for a few ales at the weekend. Billy has never had five quid before, and his question is genuine. George Jackson of Cottingham dreams first:

"It'd be two pound of good steak from the butcher down Hallgate in Cottingham, a pound of sausages, two pints each for me and our Sam in the King Billy then back home so my mam can cook us up a supper. I'd bring home a half bottle of brandy as well. There's a redheaded lass works in the office at the haulage firm behind the lumber yard, I'd ask her out for a walk and a cup of tea at the café on Finkle street, if I had five quid." It has begun to rain again outside and in the darkness under the white electric light, the three men listen to the hammering on the window and the spray of the ocean as it washes onto the deck. They consider the image George dreamed up there of a steak dinner and a red headed lass. George did not dream he would say this.

Tommy Woods of Tyne Street, Hessle Road goes next.

"If I didn't have to pay that big bastard, it'd be a trip out on the train to Hornsea beach and an ice-cream. I'd take me mam and sister. I'd buy one of those little windmill things you hold in your hand that spin, and a balloon. We'd have fizzy pop on the train back home and fish and chips too. There's a pub called the Star and Garter on Hessle Road, a real place not too far away from the docks with a piano player and warm ale, there's dancing sometimes and a good time to be had, I bet. I've never been in." The *Kestrel* bumps over the waves below as the bow breaks the water. George can smell the ice-cream and the vinegar from the fish and chips, and he can see the lights of the pub in the darkness, and hear the tinkling of the piano from within. Big Billy goes next:

"I'd give my mam a pound note, and I'd put on my best Sunday clothes with a clean cap and a neckerchief of red. I'd be all fresh and smelling nice. I'd walk across the fields, past Mickelson Farm with his barking dogs, and to the Pipe and Glass pub in front of Dalton House. I'd go in through the front door and they'd say—'you can piss off thee, Billy Petersen, you can piss off because you'll have nowt to pay for the ale you'll sup,' and I'll reach into my best jacket pocket and fetch out a clean, bright one pound note and I'll say 'I'll pay with this'. She'll have a face like shite will the landlady. Then I'll sup, three to five ales an hour, standing there at the bar next to all the posh folk. Should any of those fancy looking lads who work the livery yard say owt that I considered rude, I'd take them outside and clobber them round their heads. I'd take them all on if I had to, whole pub if needed. When it's done, I'd walk back over the fields and past Mickelson Farm with his barking dogs, and our mam would have made us a fish supper."

It is the most they have ever heard Billy speak. For a moment, the three men see it: the orange sunset behind the thatched roof of the Pipe and Glass pub, the rich lads who work at the livery yard swarming Billy as he belts one of them across the cheek with a right hook, and wrestles another one from his back into the dusty ground before clobbering another. It is perfect.

The electric light above them flickers. The cold and the sea make them dream. From above they hear the ship's bell clanging out into the night air calling them to work. The first mate, John Grace, will want them to haul up the net to see what they have caught. The dream is over. George stands first.

"Five quid," he repeats to the other men sitting down and they both grin up at him.

CHAPTER THIRTEEN

The *U-19* is once again under the frozen water. The men opened the last big tin of tuna and portioned out the meat between them. They still have some of their war bread, it's made from potato and rye, and the crew cook it on a kerosene burner up on deck when they can. The little range inside where they are supposed to prepare food is broken, like a lot of things on the *U-19*.

The men have been muttering. Krieger can hear them whispering like they always do, but it's louder than usual. What's the point in hunting a little fishing boat? Why not just fire a torpedo at it, and be on the way home? He hears Stolz whispering. He doesn't have to understand the words to know what the tall, blonde man will be saying. It will be something cruel, like the captain has lost his marbles, and if Stolz were in charge they'd have already slipped under the British blockade and be halfway back to Wilhelmshaven by now. The men are nearing the end of their patience and, truth be told, so is Krieger. Like he explained to Felix, however, he cannot let this one go. He has been entrusted to follow orders and if he decides to skip and run because it doesn't suit him, then he is no type of leader at all. Weisbach, the old skipper whose command he now has, explained that a captain has no friends on a U-boat, maybe that's why he had a dog.

When it became clear that they were not going to catch the trawler, Krieger ordered the *U-19* to dive, and they followed behind, albeit slower than before. He told Stolz that the trawler skipper would be greedy and once he thought the U-boat had gone, he'd go back to fishing. He was proved right as soon as darkness fell. In the black, winter night, they surfaced a quarter of a mile away from the big lights of the trawler and cut the engine so that Felix could get a look at it. This is where they are now.

Krieger stands in complete darkness on the bridge above

the conning tower. If there were any lights visible on the *U-19*, they'd be spotted and would lose the element of surprise they might have. He looks across the dark waters at the trawler. With his naked eye he can just make out the little men on deck hauling up their catch in the far distance under their floodlights. The sky is jet black and thick with clouds. Stolz appears behind him.

"Let's bring her around, load the bow torpedo tube and sink her, Captain," his voice is a low whisper. "The crew have had enough." Krieger turns to the taller man and looks up into the darkness of his face, he knows the eyes will be piggy and mean behind the round glasses. Krieger must nip this insolence in the bud before it grows into something nastier. He's already left it too late.

"We will neither waste a torpedo, which will be worth more than that entire boat and their catch, nor these men's lives. Do you understand?" He hears the man snort. "Question my orders one more time, Herr Stolz, and I'll have you court-marshalled." There's another snort.

"I have friends, you might be aware, Captain, who have some influence in the port back home, you do know this?" Krieger heard the man has an uncle in the Kaiserliche Marine, but this is the first time Stolz has used such a tone on him.

"Is that a threat, or are you using it in your defence? Perhaps you'd like to tell me about how big your brother is or hide behind your mother's skirt."

"It's simply a fact, Captain. Your lack of direction on this trip has been noted and we are all aware this is your first command. Perhaps the reason you stall is that you understand it may well be your last."

"We do not kill innocent men just because you wish to be back for your mother's home cooking, Stolz. Stand your responsibilities like a man. This vessel will be repaired by dawn and we will sink the trawler then, do not speak to me of it again." There is another huff in the darkness from the tall man.

"This war will be won by those who can do what needs to be done, Krieger. If you don't have the stomach for it, then perhaps it's you who should be running home to your mother's cooking." Stolz's voice is ugly and rude. He believes he has the better of Krieger because of his whispering with the other crew. They have been at sea too long. They are hungry. The freezing water is relentless. The U-19 is hell to stay aboard. Any body of men would feel the same.

Krieger steps back in the darkness behind Stolz on the bridge, he takes a deep breath, curls his hand into a fist and explodes forward with a liver punch to the first mate's side. Stolz goes down to the right with a groan and Krieger catches him before he hits the slippery metal surface of the bridge. The captain has struck with aplomb.

"You must watch your footing, Herr Stolz," whispers Krieger, as he stops him from falling, "if you're not careful, you'll go overboard." The captain cannot see the man's face in the darkness—he has given the tall, blonde officer fair warning with the strike. This is Krieger's ship and if the first officer questions orders, then the safety of everyone on board is at risk. "The next time you are insubordinate to me, I will break your pretty nose."

There are three men in the cramped engine room of the U-19. Felix is sweating and his hands are greasy with oil. He has taken this middle section of the engine apart to find the cracked cylinder head and replaced it. The other crew members have helped as best they could, like nurses assisting a skilled surgeon, they have passed him spanners and read pressure gauges for him at the far side of the engine. Felix is as skilled as they come, as a small boy back in Hamburg his father took him to see the steam trains going in and out of the docks, and the thrill of it made his chest hurt and his legs tingle. Although he is sweating through gritted teeth, Felix loves this job and loves the U-19.

"Start her up for me, Wilfred," he calls, and the man in a blue navy hat pulls down the engine lever. There's a dull hum as the diesel engine fires just below him and then a rumble. Wilfred turns up the throttle and further down where Felix stands there's movement. The case is closed so Felix can't watch the pistons spin, he listens and nods his head as he does. This is the familiar sound of the engine working as it should.

Krieger makes his way into the space through the watertight bulkhead door. He takes off his cap.

"Is she all good?" he asks.

"I think so, Captain. We'll need to get her up to full speed for a couple of hours before I can be sure, but all being well, she'll get us home." Felix wipes his greasy hands down with a rag as he stands looking up at the captain.

"We've got just under three hours till dawn, then we'll dive and move into position. As soon as the sun breaks over the horizon line, we'll be on them. It will be one last time, and then it really will be home." The captain is saying this for the assistants' benefit too, he knows they will share this information with the rest of the crew, and he hopes it will buoy their spirits. "With a bit of luck, we'll be under the blockade in twelve hours and home in a day and a half," adds Krieger. The crewman who started the engine grins under his light beard that he has not been able to shave off over the last month, his blue eyes twinkle. "Best get some rest, all of you."

Krieger lies on his bunk, with his knees bent, and his eyes facing towards the hull. There's a curtain that he can draw to get some privacy. This is more than can be said for the crew. They hot-bunk, and some of them get hammocks hung from ceiling hooks above the huge, stinking battery that powers the *U-19* underwater. Stretched out next to him is Nero with her head resting on her paws and her brown eyes blinking at him in the dim light. She is not built to be aboard a U-boat, and Krieger will not let her come along on the next trip. She is

Felix's dog. He has no real idea why she's decided to stay with him; perhaps it's the quietest place on the boat.

Stolz has the control room some twenty yards away, and Krieger is having a minute to be alone—he needs this. In his thumb and forefinger, and held up to his eyes, is a black and white picture of an elderly man and woman sitting in two chairs with a younger girl standing behind. The light cannot show that it was hot that day. They are formally dressed and their expressions are level and serious. This is Krieger's family. His sister is older now, nearly nineteen, and his grandfather has aged since this picture was taken. It is hard to do the right thing. Krieger could have turned the *U-19* round a long time ago and gone home. The man with the big moustache looks out of the picture at him—he would be proud of his grandson; Krieger knows this and that is why he's proud of himself. When he gets home there will be no need to mention what the men on the *SM U-19* have achieved, their silence will be testimony to the fight and the horror.

Tomorrow, he will put the crew of the little trawler onto their lifeboat and see them drift off as they watch their vessel slip into the freezing waves of the north water. Then, the *U-19* will turn and head south, they will dive under the British blockade and resurface miles away and speed on to Wilhelmshaven, where this vessel will live to fight another day.

The shift has changed on the *Kestrel*. George and Big Billy have gone down for a kip and Woods is about to join them. It has been a productive night and the men are weary from gutting. The hauls have been full of slippery silver cod and sometimes hake. The cutting was rotten in the freezing weather, but the sea was calm enough. They've shot the trawl over the side and morning is about to break across the horizon.

The *Kestrel* is short by a few men and so the shifts will overlap. Young Jack is back on the deck mending nets; he's already seen to the fishroom and made sure it's stacked up to his liking. Cooper and Skipper Williams are in the wheelhouse and down in the galley, Stout is smoking a cigarette waiting for water to boil. It might as well be any day while they are at the job of fishing.

Big Billy is asleep as soon as his head hits the pillow. Woods arranges his bunk before he lies down, and George is in the bucket room that is their makeshift toilet with one of his coughing fits—he is getting used to how they feel with the shivering pains and the cramps in his stomach. It takes him a few minutes to get it over with, and he makes his way to the bunk room, weak from it all as he sits down on the bottom rung of the bed. Big Billy snores in long honks through his open mouth above.

"See you in four hours," says Woods. George grins. The last thing he expected to find here were friends. They have done a very fair night's work with the fish they hauled over the side of the *Kestrel*. Woods showed them how to gut properly. It is not so complex; rather, it's more disgusting at first, then just tiresome. He hears the man lie back onto the bunk with a thud and George pulls off one of his wellies. His hands are shivering with exhaustion and cold. He swings his legs over and feels his body relax as he stretches out. It's divine.

Young Jack is a good worker. He is quick to learn and steady; because he's a kid he doesn't have any of the arrogance that older fishermen do. Back in Hull, Jack's grandmother is practically bedridden but he has an older sister who looks after the elderly woman. Jack has done a few trips on the trawlers already and he turns over the money he makes to his sister who runs the little house his grandmother has—it makes Jack feel like a man to be able to provide for them, and more of a man than his own father who he has never seen.

On the deck of the *Kestrel*, he's hung one of the nets up and is working his way through fixing any holes with the braiding needle. His eyes are keen and he is quick. In an hour or so, Skipper Williams will give the call and they'll haul in the net that the *Kestrel* is slowly dragging along the seabed behind them. He stands up to stretch his back out then walks to the starboard side of the ship so he can get a look at the sun coming up in the far distance. The sea is choppy only. The cable on the flagpole rattles in the light breeze. The funnel oozes thick black smoke from the coal furnace. The water slaps against the edge of the boat as she cuts an idle path through the sea. Jack narrows his eyes at the sun coming up.

There's a bubbling noise from just in front of him and he steps back. Under the water, the ballast tanks in the *U-19* are being pumped with air to make her rise, and, nose first, she breaks the surface of the icy blue sea. The conning tower rises before Jack's eyes and little waterfalls run from the railings— he draws his breath in horror. She is a grey sea monster coming from the deep, and Jack stands back gawping. Like the rest of the crew, he had put thoughts of this vessel out of his mind.

The hatch in the top of the conning tower opens out and two men step into the brightening morning. They have sailor's hats and rifles. This is a practiced movement for both stand either side of the opening and point their weapons onto the deck of the *Kestrel*. Almost as quick, another two men leave the hatch. In two steps, they jump off the conning tower and onto the main deck in front. They have German sailor's berets and white jumpers and their trousers are held up with braces. At the twelve pound deck gun, one of them undoes two clips on the bottom and then both sailors swing the wide barrel across and up at the deck of the *Kestrel*. Jack is aghast. It has happened so quickly that his heart has not had enough time to start pumping.

More follow with rifles. There's a tall blonde man with an officer's cap and then another smaller officer next to him appears with dark hair and a more serious face. It has taken the crew of the U-boat a minute and they are ready to attack.

Jack's eyes under his bowl haircut flitter across the deck of the U-boat opposite him. He sees the heavy wires that connect the conning tower to the bow, sees the wind blowing at the hair on the back of the dark officer's hair, and blinks as he feels the barrels of some seven rifles as well as the twelve pound deck gun pointed at him.

Krieger steps forward. There's a calm sense of power as he puts his hands on the railings of the bridge. Skipper Williams appears at the door of the wheelhouse. He is higher up than the *U-19* and looks down on the vessel with narrow eyes. The old skipper doesn't seem as shocked as he ought to be; he waits for the captain of the U-boat to react first. Krieger turns and nods to Stolz who has good English. He calls to the crew of the *Kestrel*:

"All your crew on deck." Williams holds his hand above his eyes against the sunshine coming from behind the *U-19*. He shakes his head as if he doesn't quite understand. Stolz gives a snarl and repeats.

"All crew on the deck, now," he yells. Skipper Williams wrinkles his nose. The blue cat inside the wheelhouse looks out the window at the men on the little U-boat with complete indifference, as if with their funny sticklike rifles, they are insignificant. Williams has heard about what happens in these situations. He is not going to make it easy for men who will, at best, put him adrift in a lifeboat in the middle of the frozen sea. In the face of authority, like all Hull trawlermen, he will do his very best to take the piss.

Stolz snorts as the old man does not seem to move. There are no specific rules about what to do in these situations. Their two countries are at war so Krieger could have his men spray the *Kestrel* with bullets if he so wished, but that's not his style at all. This may be a war but there are ways in which men conduct themselves. Once their respective governments come to their senses in a few months, this will all be over. Krieger will go back to first mate or even a captaincy on a freight ship and he will not have the blood of these poor English trawler men on his hands. He is not going to watch more men drowned like he did with *HMS Pathfinder*. This does not mean that Krieger is a pushover, far from it, he will injure these grumpy fishermen if he has to.

He clicks his tongue, and the two riflemen let off three shots each into the morning air. The gulls nattering at the rear of the trawler ignore the sound of it, but the blue cat looking out the window jumps to her senses and drops to the floor to hide behind the back of the door. Skipper Williams must now act, he switches the handle on the ship's telegraph to stop—this will relay the message to Cooper or Peter Everett in the engine room to cut the power. Then he reaches out and rings the big brass bell of the *Kestrel*. It clangs out in the cold early morning. This will call all the men on deck.

Billy has been asleep for about fifteen minutes. He has just hit heavy snoring, and his big mouth is open wide with his head tilted back on the pillow. One of his big boots hangs off the side of the bunk. The ship's bell clangs out in the morning. George opens one eye in the semi-darkness and pulls the blanket off his fully clothed body.

"What's going on?" he asks. Woods responds:

"Something's happened. I'll go and have a look."

"I'll do it," says George. Playing the role of big brother comes naturally because he's been doing it all his life. He swings himself off the lower bunk, slips his feet still in the same stinky socks into his wellies, and steps through to the door that is open just an inch. It's too early for George to have one of his coughing fits, as if his body is not yet ready to face the wincing pain of it. He pulls his braces over his jumper and moves to the door. As he climbs the slippery ladder up to the deck above, sharp light blinds him from the morning sun. He has not been to bed yet and it is another day. The bell rings out again. The clanging is aggressive. George comes to his senses as he makes his way round past the wheelhouse, and to the starboard side.

It takes him a minute to work out what is going on. The skipper stands on deck with his hands on his hips wearing his mucky white roll neck sweater under his coat. Next to him is John Grace, then Young Jack beside Cooper, and even Stout is up and out of the kitchen. George walks to join them and sees it, the half-submerged German U-boat sitting low in the water, with men covering its deck and conning tower. Their rifles are aimed and a big deck gun is ready to blow a hole in the *Kestrel*. George does a sharp intake of breath as he looks across at the German seamen with their funny sailor style pork pie hats and braces over their jumpers. It's as if they have come straight from a picture in a book, as if the war was not all real, until now, when they are face to face with the enemy.

"Is that everybody?" calls Stolz from the *U-19*. Skipper Williams looks down the uneven line of men and shrugs his shoulders as if he doesn't know or care. There are two men missing, Woods and Big Billy. Stolz does not want this to go on for too long and he does not like the arrogance of these fishermen. Apart from the boy, the crew do not seem bothered by the appearance of the *U-19*, as if it's more of an inconvenience for them. They are scared, of course, but their natural response to authority is indifference and dumb insolence.

"You will launch your lifeboat," calls Stolz. "You will row here to us." He points to the deck of the *U-19*. This is how it works. They have done it before. The trawlermen come over in their lifeboat and, like men about to be shot, they stand on the deck of the *U-19* and watch as Stolz and his men sail back over to the trawler in the same boat. The Germans will ransack it first for whatever they can find, fresh food, bottles of booze, trinkets that the men have left behind and anything else. Once they're satisfied they've got as much as they can, Stolz will slip down into the engine room and do something unpleasant.

He'll find the seacocks or valves that cool the engine and just open them up to flood the ship, or he'll leave a bomb in the engine room. It will take time. Once Stolz is back on the *U-19*, the English trawlermen will return to their little lifeboat and drift away into the water to take their chances against the sea.

Skipper Williams makes his way to the stern of the *Kestrel* and the other men follow down the side of the wheelhouse. There's no particular rush. At the lifeboat, Williams nods to Grace and Cooper. They untie the little vessel from where it's secured to the deck. Jack and George help carry it to the side of the *Kestrel*, and they lower it into the water on ropes at the fore and aft. The men work without speaking under the silence of the German rifles and the big deck gun that points at the hull of the *Kestrel*. Gulls squawk behind and the ship creaks in the choppy water, the sun is coming up behind the *U-19*.

John Grace feels his stomach tighten and his legs weaken. The vessel they are lowering into the water is not particularly seaworthy, it's for emergencies, but what does it matter? There is no reason for John Grace to go back to Hull at all if he is not going to get paid, because he will not be able to resolve the debt he has built up at the gambling table. He might as well be lost under these freezing cold northern waves.

George Jackson thinks of his brother asleep back in Cottingham. There is nothing George can do but follow the orders of the men with rifles and hope that they will be picked up by another boat. He has learned that the sea is fickle and wilful; out here George has no choice in his actions. If he makes it home, he will take some decisions back into his own hands. He'll go down to that conscription office for a word with the doctor who would not allow him to sign up. It will be a special conversation, for out of all this, George knows his brother will not survive if he goes to war alone. He will have to go with him, and it will be his duty to do so. George often wondered what life would be like with freedom from the burden of Sam, and now he knows; the burden is the definition of who he is.

Cooper lowers the lifeboat through rough, soot-stained hands. The *Kestrel* is his home. He knows how to trim the coal better than anyone, he understands the way she rocks on the waves and dips in a storm. He likes the top bunk in the corner of the crew's quarters. If he makes it back to Hull, Cooper will have to go through it all again to find another trawler to sail aboard. There will be question after question by the skippers and the first mate, they will want him to remove his cap and have a wash. Cooper will again have to hide what he has hidden for so long. It will be a right pain.

Peter Everett examines the hull and the build of the *U-19* as the other crew lower the lifeboat. It is smaller than he imagined it would be, and it sits low in the water with the deck only a yard or so above the waves. It must be cramped inside, he thinks. Everett knows that the torpedoes are fired out the front, and it is strange to think that ratty looking men such as these would have destroyed a cruiser like the *HMS Pathfinder*. On the bridge looking through the railings is a little black and tanned dog with a long, regal face and pointed ears. Peter Everett is not afraid anymore, his body is too tired; and in the short time he has spent with these trawlermen he has begun to copy their acceptance of death. There is no point in shitting yourself before you have to. Maybe that's what he's been doing ever since they dragged him out of the water between the wreckage of the *Pathfinder*.

Skipper Williams also looks across to the *U-19* bobbing on the water opposite. The Germans are pale and underfed. Their eyes are hungry. They're unshaven and dirty with an edge of madness to them. Williams considers the smaller of the two officers on the conning tower with his arms folded, this must be the captain. He watches his men lower the lifeboat into the water. The old skipper is not frightened of the sea, not at all, she will not see him drowned because she is too cruel. The men of the *Kestrel* will freeze to death or starve out on the open sea, but she will not have Skipper Williams under the waves to die. He steps away from the men and to the side of the *Kestrel* so he can call across at the Germans.

"I forgot my cat," he shouts. They hear him but there is no movement from the sailors. "I think she's gone below. I need to get her." Williams is not asking permission; he is stating a fact.

"Your crew are out here, Captain, remember that," calls back Stolz. Williams nods and makes his way down the deck on bandy but quick legs. He knows where the animal will be. The old man with his mucky roll-necked jumper gets to the hatch, opens it up, and climbs down the ladder to the sleeping quarters. He is slow and methodical. In the darkness at the bottom, he pushes open the door to the bunkroom.

Woods stands there in front of him. Big Billy is still in the top bunk and snoring with his boot hanging over the side.

"What's happening?"

"We're being ordered off the boat," mutters Skipper Williams under his breath. "That U-boat has surfaced next to us. If you don't want to be sunk, I suggest you get out on deck as well. Where's the cat?" Woods thinks these words over.

"I'm not going home without a full fishroom, Skipper," he whispers. "There's no point in going back if I'll not get paid. My mam told me."

"Suit yourself then, lad. Ten minutes and they'll be all over this boat." Skipper Williams pretends he does not care. The men who sail under his command are not his children or his responsibility; they follow his orders only because they want to catch the most fish they can and get home quickly. He knows that Woods will follow rather than die. This is how folk are. "Where's the cat?" repeats the skipper.

"In the corner," says Woods. Williams strides into the darkness and to the space under the bunk. He squats, reaches out his hand, and drags out the blue cat by the scruff of her neck. She is thankful for it and he puts her over his right shoulder as he makes his way to the door and the ladder to the deck above. He turns back to Woods.

"You better wake that big bastard up as well, if you don't want to get shot, or drowned, or both." With one of his wiry arms on the ladder and the other securing the blue cat on his shoulder, Williams climbs up to the bright light of the deck above.

In the semi-dark of the bunk room, Woods feels the weight of the *Kestrel* sway with the waves below. He blinks. Big Billy snores yet on the bunk next to him. If the Germans put them adrift then the *Kestrel* will be scuttled, it will not return fish to Hull and if by some miracle the crew are picked up and they make it back to port, they will not be paid. Woods will not get his five pounds, and he will not be able to pay his cousin. The words of his mother ring in his ears yet. There is no point in Woods returning home if he has nothing. It will be another failure. Just like his life has been a failure so far ever since his father and older brother died at sea, and ever since he fell into the fishroom of a trawler and snapped his ankle. Perhaps he has been a failure ever since he first opened his eyes when he came out of his mother's stomach.

There's no point in him giving up. Woods is not going to follow the skipper up to the deck and the Germans.

He'll not be leaving the *Kestrel* and all the fish they have just caught without a fight.

CHAPTER FOURTEEN

"Is that all the crew?" yells Stolz again from the *U-19*. His accent is clearly foreign but understandable, even if it is lost in the wind somewhat. The men of the *Kestrel* have still not left their ship. They wait at the port side with the little lifeboat in the water just below them. None of them respond to the question. Skipper Williams now stands with the blue cat over one of his shoulders but the same angry, steel look in his eyes.

"If there's some man hiding, he will be shot. He will be shot or he will sink with the ship," bellows Stolz over the waves. The crew of the *Kestrel* look back at him with blank faces. Stolz has good English; for a time, he sailed on a merchant cruiser between Bremerhaven, Calais, London and sometimes North America. Some of the crew were British and Stolz learned from necessity. Krieger steps forward towards his first officer.

"It's a small ship," he whispers, "this will be all of them."

"Seven men?" mutters Stolz back.

"And a cat. They're unarmed. These are fishermen. Order them across on their little boat and let's get this over with." Stolz agrees with his superior. He calls across to the crew some thirty yards away:

"Get on the boat," he yells, pointing down to the lifeboat bobbing on the waters next to the *Kestrel*. John Grace and Peter Everett hold it steady while Skipper Williams climbs down the rope ladder with the cat on his shoulder. He is lithe for an old man. This is the North Sea, without anchors down, the two vessels are beginning to drift slightly apart. The bow of the *Kestrel* is turning in the choppy water so it points at an angle closer to the *U-19*. It's never plain sailing.

The rest of the men board the lifeboat with John Grace last. Peter Everett holds out his hand to help the portly Scouser onto the little boat. Cooper and Young Jack take up the rowing but with a few strokes, it's clear the boy is not strong enough to manage. George takes over and they begin the journey across to the *U-19*. Skipper Williams sits at the bow but does not take his eyes from the two German officers standing on the bridge of the grey U-boat.

"What about the others?" whispers Jack from next to him.

"It's their choice, kid," he answers. Jack looks around at the stone faces of the men in the lifeboat with him. It feels wrong to leave the *Kestrel* for the danger of this wooden craft.

It takes them a few minutes to row across to the *U-19*. The water is rough, and without an engine to power them, George and Cooper feel the strain of the waves against the oars. As soon as they are ten yards away, a crew member from the *U-19* throws across a line and John Grace uses it to haul the boat in with his powerful arms.

The German crew are not unkind. A leathery hand is offered to Young Jack, and he steps up and off the boat onto the long deck of the *U-19*. The sailors make room for him to walk right to the end. The rest of the crew follow: Cooper clambers aboard, Stout struggles to make the step up because of his gut, George goes next then Peter Everett who is no longer shaking. John Grace struggles also and finally, Skipper Williams makes the step with that blue cat over his shoulder clinging on for its life. As soon as they are on board, a detachment of four crew hop into the lifeboat with Stolz stepping on last. They begin the journey back to the *Kestrel* as it bobs lonely on the waters, with whisps of smoke coming off the stack that is still burning coal.

Krieger considers the men standing on the deck of his U-boat. They look oddly pathetic lined up to the end of the vessel with their ragged clothes and varying heights. In other encounters they have done much the same with crews who were larger than this one. Rifles are no longer pointed at the trawlermen of the *Kestrel* for it's clear that they are wretched and pitiful, from the old man skipper to the kid who should be at school. George Jackson feels his morning convulsions coming over him, his shoulders bend as his chest begins to spasm in the cough that has been with him for the last six months. Like a cat hacking up a fur ball, he splutters and barks, his eyes are narrowed in pain. He manages to get his handkerchief to his mouth, and the coughing comes stronger and harder as he drops to one knee. John Grace grabs one of the braces over his thick jumper to stop him from going overboard. He splutters on past a few minutes, and for a time his hollow coughing is the only sound out there, as the German sailors row to the *Kestrel*, and the men standing on the deck of the *U-19* watch George struggle. Krieger sees the blood all over the handkerchief from the trawlerman's mouth when he finally stops coughing. The German captain has seen this before, his grandfather had it – it is tuberculosis probably. He is sorry for the man, genuinely.

John Grace helps George to stand.

"You'll need to see a doctor when you get back," he whispers. George stares up at him with cold, red eyes.

There are four men on the rowing boat moving towards the *Kestrel* and, for the German sailors, it feels good to have space around them and the open sky above. Stolz sits up front as they cut through the mid-sized waves. The men who row are strong and happy to be outside even if it is cold. The oars against their muscles feel sweet and real and the sharp wind is fresh rather than cold to faces that have spent weeks in the wet mould of the *U-19*.

They are eager too about what they might find on the fishing boat, of course there will be fresh cod and haddock but there may also be cheese, butter, even eggs.

They arrive at the *Kestrel* on the port side. Stolz manages to throw up a rope and hook it around the gallows where the trawler usually hauls in her nets. The waves make this more difficult but Stolz is an experienced seaman, he knows how to wait in time for the water then pulls them in with the waves.

He gets the lifeboat tight to the side of the *Kestrel* and knots it there while another sailor fixes the stern in much the same way. There's excitement here.

The first two men clamber up and over the rails onto the side of the ship like monkeys. Stolz goes next. He's taller and less lithe than these two. The last sailor will stay with the little lifeboat.

On the deck the smell of fish is strong. The two men begin down past the trawl winch to the wheelhouse. Stolz barks an order at them:

"Patience, please gentlemen." They look back at him and grin from under their sailor's hats. They have orders to stay together, it is safer that way. Stolz does not expect that there will be anyone on this trawler, and within the hour this rusty vessel will be on its way to the bottom of the cold sea. They'll check the wheelhouse first.

Stolz climbs the ladder upwards and goes through the little open door. There's the wheel and the engine telegraph, and the skipper's tin cup half full of tea on top of the compass. Under those round glasses, his blue eyes inspect the room for anything they can take. On the floor there's an iron bucket, a spanner, a wet newspaper page and a single rubber wellington boot. There's nothing here.

On the deck the men go aft towards the galley where there's another ladder leading down to the crew's bunk room. The first sailor opens up the hatch to the darkness. He peers inside before he considers going down. These bunk rooms are good to search, trawlerman often keep trinkets here they don't want to wear or use on deck. There may also be bottles of spirits or foodstuffs, rings, chains, or saucy photos that they are hiding from the other members of the crew.

The first sailor goes down the ladder, then the next follows who has brought a torch on Stolz's orders. Stolz himself has removed his handgun from the holster at his side, you never know what will be down there. Back in the mess hall at

Wilhelmshaven, he heard tales of dogs being left in holds as well as ducks or geese—all of these can bite. Before he goes down, he does a check of the boat around him and sees the *U-19* some hundred yards off the starboard bow as each vessel drifts in the currents. It's strange to see a thing he knows from so far away, but there is cheer in this tall German man's heart for the thrill of ransacking through the trawlerman's gear. There will also be the joy of going into a strange engine room and opening up the seacocks to let the ocean flood in. Pistol drawn, Stolz turns and descends down the ladder with one hand holding onto the rungs.

In the little corridor, there is a line of doors on one side. Stolz motions with his head to the far one.

"What you find is not yours to keep," he barks, "every man on the *U-19* has a rightful share." He knows they will keep anything small that they can slip into their pockets, it's a reward for putting yourself in harm's way. Stolz will do the same. It takes a minute for them to search the Skipper's quarters at the far end. One of the sailors grins in the half light, he has a bottle of what looks like cognac. Stolz grins too.

Back in the corridor, Stolz turns to the first door and pushes it open to the gloom inside. This is the bunk room; he can tell by the smell. Here they'll find any jewellery these fishermen won't wear when they work or maybe pictures of their wives and girlfriends. Stolz finds himself grinning again as he steps inside. It seems a pity that those poor fishermen will be left to drift out in the frozen sea, and now he thinks about this, he understands that Krieger was right not to sink them in cold blood. Standing in the doorway, Stolz finds his eyes adjusting to the light. He sees the clothes and boots strewn on the floor along with newspapers and bottles.

"Get that torch in here," he calls, and the sailor brings the bright yellow beam against the far bulkhead. It illuminates the corners of the room and there, standing like a huge waxwork model in the yellow light, stands the figure of a man.

It's Big Billy.

Stolz has been in fights before, of course. At the military academy, they boxed in shorts with heavy padded gloves. He's had scuffles in bars with drunks, and a tussle with a big Latvian once at a camp north of Bremen. Stolz is more of a thinker than a fighter; that's why he's an officer. He's read books on ancient tactics about how Alexander the Great overpowered the far superior Persian army, and how Napoleon outmanoeuvred his opponents yet was defeated at Waterloo. None of this has prepared him for the big and powerful East Riding fist that comes in a perfect arc from Big Billy out of the darkness. The knuckles describe a smooth angle as he swings for the tall German officer who is not as tall as he is. They connect with his cheek and cut him down like straw under the blade of a scythe.

Ten minutes before, Woods woke Big Billy by shaking him. He did not stop even after the huge man had told him to 'piss off' more times than was reasonable. In whispered tones, Woods explained that up above, the crew were being put into the lifeboat and that the German U-boat was back. He told Billy to get up and get on deck if he valued his life because soon enough, the German navy would be on board to ransack the ship and then sink it. Billy usually takes a minute to come to his senses after he's woken up and so, he did not process the information right away, even though Woods explained it again.

"I'm not going," said Billy as he laid there in his bunk. He does not do what he's told, doesn't Big Billy. He will often do what is right, but he won't do as he's asked. This was true for the petty school master back in Etton, the livery yard boss on the farm where he worked, the Beverley landlord at the White Horse pub or Billy's own father who, even now, lies dead in a coffin ready for his funeral a week next Tuesday.

When Woods left, Billy got himself up and pushed open the bunk room door. He crept up the ladder and peered out the hatch to the light of the morning. There was no sign of Woods at all. Billy didn't climb right out, he just went far enough to catch a glimpse of the grey U-boat low in the water, and all those German naval soldiers with their rifles pointed at something. Billy hid back down in the bunk room. In the darkness he ran his hand over the stubble beginning across his chin. If he went up on deck, they would shoot him. Billy decided to wait for the boarding party before he made a move.

Back in the darkness of the bunkroom, Big Billy has belted the thin German officer across his cheek and knocked him against the bunk on the other side of the room. He is about to follow up with a left to the shapes that move towards him, but these are men, the like of which, Billy has not fought before. The German navy does not let just anyone take a position aboard a U-boat. The crew are not like the piss-head farm hands who drink in the Light Dragoon at Etton; these are trained men who have studied the art of fighting in boxing or hand to hand combat.

The first sailor ducks his head, and Billy's heavy left fist finds nothing but air as it whistles past. The other one, holding the torch, shines it right into Billy's face to blind him. Then the first sailor rushes forward, catches Billy by the middle and they both crash against the bulkhead. There are grunts and yells in the darkness. Fists fly. Billy grabs the sailor's head at his chest and the torch whirls as the second sailor moves in. Stolz comes to his senses, and searches for his glasses on the floor next to him.

There's no glory to this kind of fighting. None of the combatants have had a drink. There's been no exchange of unpleasantries beforehand. Billy has not had his heritage questioned. It is only the struggle between men who are afraid of each other, and also, afraid that they might die. It is a new sensation to Billy—these men who have him pinned against the bulkhead are not scared of him and, they will kill him if they have to. This is war.

Stolz finds his glasses, and with shaking hands places them on his face once more. He can sense the men struggling in the room close to him. As he is getting to his feet, he raises the Luger pistol above his head then fires off a shot. The noise rings out around the tiny room and combined with the attack of the two tough German sailors, Billy covers up his face with his arms to stop the punches. He is trying to give up.

"I'm done," he yells in his defence. The sailors do not waste any time with him. The one who has him pinned to the bulkhead, steps back and delivers a sharp liver punch that drops Billy to his knees. As soon as he falls, the sailors draw him up again and twist his arms so that his hands are half-way up his back. These are professional fighters and there are no mistakes. The light from the torch shines on the blonde man's head, and now he is standing, Stolz brings the barrel of the gun into Billy's temple so it digs into his flesh. There's a snarl on this officer's bruised face. His finger finds the trigger on the Luger.

"Don't kill him, Comrade," comes a whisper from the sailor holding the torch light. "He's just a fisherman." The comment makes Stolz's anger seem pathetic, as if he's upset with some sort of wild beast. It's a reminder too, that Krieger, even though he is not here, is a Christian and commands these level and strong sailors who manage the *U-19*. They are more like their captain than this petty officer.

"He'd have killed me," mutters Stolz as he pulls the pistol back from the Yorkshireman's temple. The sailor who grips Billy's neck responds:

"He has the fear of death, Comrade, that's all. You'd have done the same."

CHAPTER FIFTEEN

Up on the deck of the *Kestrel,* one of the sailors stands guard behind Big Billy who is on his knees with his hands behind his head. There's a gash across the big man's temple where the sailor belted him and his face is grey with the cold. Billy is not used to losing fist fights, and the experience is sobering for him. It may even be healthy. The sailor holds Stolz's Luger pointing at the big man's back. They're not going to kill Billy, but they aren't going to take any shite from him either.

Confident that there won't be any more trouble, Stolz and the other soldier search the rest of the ship. After they've been through the bunk room, they quickly move to the galley kitchen. The sailor fills two buckets with stuff—there's cheese, a sack of potatoes, a bag of coffee, butter, leeks, and carrots. He turns his nose up at any cans and there's no fresh meat left, but that doesn't matter. Down in the fishroom of this trawler will be as much silvery cod as the whole crew could eat many times over. Stolz has ordered the man to empty the pantry first and then go to the fishroom to fill a sack with fresh fish. Stolz himself is going down to the engine room to sink the ship— his favourite part of the job.

Stolz climbs through a hatch and down the dirty ladder to the engine. At the bottom of the rungs, he examines his surroundings. There's the boiler next to him and a temperature gauge dial on the outside beside the flap where they shovel in coal. It's all red hot. To the right is the darkness of the coal room and he marvels at just how much of the stuff they have left. It's a pity and a waste that he'll have to send this all to the bottom of the ocean.

Stolz's feet crunch on bits of coal as he walks round to the engine room past the boiler—there she is. There's the hum from the engine and the hissing from one of the cylinders, but the shaft that drives the propellor is motionless. Stolz can see from the little dials that there's still pressure in the engines. He looks over and across at the mass of pipes that carry water and steam. He doesn't pretend to understand, but he knows enough.

At the bottom of a big white pipe there's a valve. This could be what he's looking for, the cooling pump. He squats down and begins to undo the handwheel. It's stiff at first but as he loosens it, water begins to run in. This part of the *Kestrel* is below the ocean level, and this is the pump that draws seawater up to cool the engine when it's too hot. He continues to turn till seawater begins belching from the opening and within a few seconds the floor is wet against his boots. Stolz stands and watches it come through.

There's no real need to waste equipment when sinking a ship is this easy. In ten minutes, the water will be up to his knees and in another twenty, the room will be so compromised that this old trawler will sink. This should give Stolz and his crew more than enough time to board the lifeboat and row away. He stands back and is pleased with himself. He walks round to the boiler and the ladder where he first entered.

There's more.

The *U-19* and her crew have come a long way in a few short weeks. This will be their last kill, and once they are under the British blockade off Scotland, they will be home free. Stolz wants to treat the men to a little show—it's all they deserve and it's so easy to manage.

From his belt, he pulls out a long device that looks a little like a potato masher. This is a stielhandgranate, a bomb that can be thrown at the enemy. Stolz has an idea how to use it as a back-up here. He opens the little hatch to the boiler, places the stick grenade flat, then closes the hatch back up. It will take a while for the components inside the grenade to get hot enough but when they do, it will explode. Back in the military academy the munitions expert explained that a grenade next to a fire was a pretty good way to make a timed bomb. He grins when he thinks about the explosion, and how they will see it from the deck of the *U-19*. He thinks of how the crew will grin, and smile, and clap when they watch the boiler blow up and take out the whole of the back end of the trawler. It will be a sight. Stolz gives himself a congratulatory smile as he goes up the ladder to the deck above.

Woods has been laid on top of the coal for twenty minutes. He wriggled a bit at first because the uneven rocks dug into his back but now he's comfortable. He knows there is nobody in the wheelhouse above and that he is alone on the *Kestrel* until German navy sailors arrive to sink the ship. He couldn't get through to Billy that the Germans were about to board, and so he left him there. Big Billy knows how to look after himself, he hopes.

It has given him time to put the events of his life into perspective. Tommy Woods has considered how things could have been different many times before. If he had not fallen into that fishroom and broken his foot, he would have become a trawlerman proper like his father. He would not have had to stay with his cousin Mathews and he would be someone, unlike the man he is today. What did he think was going to happen on this trip? Did he imagine it would be easy? Did he think he could just work, collect his five quid, then go home and pay off his fat cousin? Woods knows he is unlucky. He knows that whatever he touches goes wrong. It is exhausting but he has kept a smile on his face as long as he can. Laid there on the coal looking up at the ceiling in the darkness with the soot in his nostrils, Woods feels himself beginning to despair as he has never really done before.

He closes his eyes and drifts. He feels the waves of the sea under him slapping against the iron sides of the *Kestrel*, senses the cold water beneath; and deep in the darkness of the ocean, he feels the slippery, silver cod fish swimming together with their eyes wide in the pitch black. He hears the noise of the hatch opening above and then footsteps coming down the ladder. His eyes open. He lifts his head, and is about to call out, when he realises this might be a German soldier. Woods holds his breath. He sits up in the darkness and hears the man walk through into the engine room. Whoever it is doesn't stop there long before they come back through, open and then close the boiler hatch, and make their way back up the ladder.

Woods lies down for a minute. Curiosity catches hold of him. He wonders what has happened to the other members of the *Kestrel*, and what has happened to Billy. He swallows. He is not a man who gives up. It's not in his nature. Like his father and big brother who are lost to the sea, Tommy Woods worries about others too much. This is why he hates his fat cousin, Mathews, and why he blames himself when, in the middle of the night he hears the man calling to his mother, and she goes to him. Tommy Woods can hear the squeak of the bed. Probably the whole house can. He promised that one day when he was powerful enough, he'd do something to stop it. Maybe that day will never come now, but he cannot just lay flat and wait to die.

He climbs out of the coal house to the opening that he crawled through, and then stands at the bottom of the ladder looking at the hatch to the boiler. Woods does not know that behind it, there is a German stick grenade, and the chemicals inside are warming up already. He looks down and sees water gathering at his boots, then follows it round to the engine room where he sees it pumping out from the valve that Stolz opened three minutes before. Woods bends down and tightens it back up. The water turns to a trickle and then stops. There's still two inches of the North Sea on the engine room floor, but the *Kestrel* will not be sinking now.

Tommy Woods looks over the motionless steam engine in much the same way as Stolz did a few minutes previously. Perhaps all the roads he has taken so far have led him here,

150

the fall in the fishroom and the years on the dockside back in Hull. What if, already, he is the only man left onboard the *Kestrel*. He sees sense like he always does. If Woods doesn't get himself off this trawler, then he'll be killed. How will that help his mam and his sisters back in Tyne Street? It'll mean they'll be trapped with fat cousin Mathews forever, and in actual fact, Tommy Woods who limps down the street with a wooden foot is better than no Tommy Woods at all—at least he gets some work on the trawlers.

Time for him to come clean. He'll have to go up on deck and show himself. If they've already left, he'll have to wave them down, and hope to bastard God above that they come back for him before they sink the ship.

Woods pushes open the hatch just by an inch so he can peer out onto the deck. The wind is at once sharp and the morning is bright. He doesn't see any movement on any side of the *Kestrel*, so he pushes it open a little more and checks again. If he goes out there too quickly, he might get shot.

The *Kestrel* and the *U-19* have drifted a little apart and the long grey vessel lies a couple of hundred yards off the starboard bow. Woods can see there are men standing on the deck that is low in the water. There's the white hair of Skipper Williams next to John Grace and the rest of the *Kestrel* crew.

In the space between the two craft is the lifeboat. Two sailors are rowing with another at the front and one at the back. They have plundered the *Kestrel*, and the little boat is full of sacks from the kitchen. Sitting facing his own ship, is Big Billy. There's blood running down his face from the gash on his head, and his eyes are calm under his straight blonde hair ruffled by the sea breeze. He sees Woods peeping out from behind the side of the wheelhouse and he grins to show the gap in his front teeth. The sailor guarding him with the pistol notices him smile at something on the deck of the *Kestrel*; he turns to look, but Woods has already dipped back out of sight in fear. The sailor figures that Billy must be taking the piss.

Behind the wheelhouse, Woods rests with his back to the bulkhead to think. What is he to do? He swallows. If he shows himself on the deck to the U-boat, they'll most likely shoot him but if he doesn't, they'll probably pound a big hole in the hull with that deck gun, and he'll go down with the ship.

He'll have to get a grip of himself.

Bold as brass, Tommy Woods of Tyne Street, Hessle Road, steps around the side of the wheelhouse and walks towards the fore of the ship so that he's in clear view of the *U-19*. His nostrils are flared and he holds his hands up and out so that they can see that he's no threat. As he gets to the edge of the *Kestrel*, one of the sailors on board the *U-19* spots him. The soldier brings the Gewehr 98 bolt-action rifle to his face and his finger goes to the trigger. It is instinct that makes him shoot, and the bullet ricochets off the wheelhouse Woods stands in front of, making the trawlerman fall and scramble back behind it.

"There's a man on board," calls the sailor. Krieger saw the figure as well. He puts his binoculars to his eyes to scan the deck for any movement. In front of them, Stolz and his rowboat have just reached the *U-19*. It's not like Krieger to reprimand one of his officers in front of the crew, but he cannot help himself.

"You've left one of those poor bastards aboard," he calls down to Stolz. The blonde man stands where he is at the stern, turns to look back at the *Kestrel*, and then turns to the captain.

"There was nobody on board."

"You didn't look properly." Stolz's face reddens. The sailor at the bow of the lifeboat has caught a rope from his shipmate and is beginning to pull the little vessel in.

"You'll go back," says Krieger. Stolz's chin quivers.

"I opened the seacock in the engine room, Captain, and I put a grenade in the furnace." It's embarrassing to say this in front of the crew, for Stolz, it is not that he has left a man aboard the stricken trawler, but that he has failed to complete his duties properly. "She'll be under the water by the time we row back."

Krieger's brown eyes are dark when he looks down on his first officer.

Skipper Williams watches as the Germans unload the sacks of food they took from the *Kestrel*. There are smiles all round from the U-boat sailors at this. They beam at the two buckets of fresh fish, and the cheese, the sack of potatoes, and the bottle of cognac they found in the officer's quarters. Williams gives a light snarl—this is his. The crew of the *Kestrel* saw the figure of Woods on the deck of their ship as well. They heard the rifle shot, and then witnessed the captain bellowing at his officer in German.

Once the sailors are off, Krieger steps forward and points at the lifeboat meaning that Williams and his men should get back on board. Young Jack goes first while John Grace holds the rope Stolz handed to him.

The captain of the U-boat looks down from the bridge on the conning tower from under his white cap. "Goodbye," he says. His English is not so good.

"You could spare us a bullet each," says Williams as he faces the U-boat commander above. "We must be six hundred miles north of Scotland in winter. There'll not be a boat to pick us up. We'll drift till we starve or freeze."

"You have your lives," says Stolz from in front of his captain.

"What about our lad you left on board our ship. What's to become of him?" asks Williams.

"He had enough time to leave. It's his fault, I'm afraid." Stolz has the turn of phrase of the English, that apologetic tone that is not really an apology at all. Skipper Williams should not be arguing with these soldiers; he should be thankful that he has the chance to sail away, but he cannot

153

help himself, the bile, and the anger from all the years comes back up like acid reflux from his stomach. He points past Stolz to the captain on the bridge above.

"You're a bastard coward," he yells. Williams is angry that this man is not prepared to finish them off. "You've not seen the bloody job through."

Krieger looks down at this thin skipper from the bridge. He understands his frustration, but he will not kill these men. If God should choose to take them, that is another matter. Besides, there is every chance they will survive, a ship could be just over the horizon to pick them up. Skipper Williams gets into the lifeboat last, and he stands at the bow with the cat over his shoulder looking at Krieger. George uses one of the oars to push them away from the U-boat.

"I am sorry about your man," calls Krieger. It is the best English he can manage. He means Woods. "My officer left a bomb in the engine room."

As they drift into the ocean away from the *U-19*, Williams stands motionless. He continues glaring up at the German captain with a look of distain across his miserable and weathered face. Krieger holds the stare. The German captain feels remorse. There is still a man on board the *Kestrel*, but it has passed beyond his control with that bomb Stolz says is on board.

Williams feels the claws of his cat over his shoulder. If it were the other way round, and he were the captain of a U-boat, he would have already sunk the *Kestrel* with everyone on it. He would be here to get the job done, not fanny around rescuing part of the crew just so he could nick their cognac and hold his head high that he had done the right thing.

The gash on his forehead has stopped bleeding but Billy looks pale as he sits opposite the filthy figure of Eric Cooper. They are just a few yards off the *U-19* and moving away on the row strokes of John Grace and George Jackson.

"What happened to Woods?" asks Cooper.

"I dunno," answers Billy. "I belted one of them—that officer but they would have shot me if I'd battered the other two." Billy doesn't have to explain.

Cooper turns back to the *Kestrel* drifting away on the ocean. She is a lonely sight with nobody on board and the trimmer moves a few seats down the rowboat so that he's nearer to Williams.

"We'll go back for him, Skipper," says Cooper. The old man looks over his shoulder.

"It's his own bloody fault," he mutters. "We'll have to put as much distance as we can between us and that trawler. When it goes down, if we're too close, we'll go with it." John Grace puts more effort into his rowing and George is already flagging with his eyes drooping. Billy moves to take over.

"He's done for if he's still on there," says Cooper.

"We're all done for," says Skipper Williams. He turns to the crew on the lifeboat and behind him is the outline of the *U-19* with her men busy on the deck. Billy and John Grace row. Cooper sits next to the skipper. Young Jack and George sit beside Peter Everett who is still not shaking. The fat cook has lit a cig. Their faces are sour as they look up at the skipper. He could tell them that it won't be so bad, that it will only be a few hours of drifting before they're picked up, that they have enough supplies inside the lifeboat for a week or more. Williams is not the sort to sugar coat anything. The less he says about Woods the better, but he can't help it.

"I told that kid they'd sink the ship with him on board."

"What did he say?" This is John Grace.

"He said he wasn't getting off. He said if he didn't get home and get his money, then it wasn't worth him going back to Hull at all."

Skipper Williams has a nasty taste in his mouth as he says this. Back home in his big house on the Boulevard, there's a two foot long safe in his library that only he knows the combination for. Inside, there are stacks of notes that Williams has made over his career—well more than the miserly payment Woods would have expected to receive when he got home.

"I thought he was taking the piss," adds the old man. "I thought he'd be right behind me." It is out of character for Skipper Williams to say anything wistful, but here he is, set adrift on the north waters in a lifeboat with his crew and they will be hundreds of miles off the Scottish or Icelandic coast. He turns to the *Kestrel*, and sees the funnel still smoking, the trawl winch and the empty wheelhouse with the door open. She should start to go down any minute now, and if she doesn't, the Germans will begin with their guns.

Woods was a good lad, a bloody fool, but a good lad just the same. Skipper Williams sits down at the bow of the lifeboat and puts the big blue cat on his knee.

He gives a great big sigh.

CHAPTER SIXTEEN

Krieger looks across at the trawler bobbing on the water. He puts his binoculars to his eyes and scans the deck. The crew of the fishing ship are rowing away with their angry, white-haired skipper muttering. It's all going to plan. The U-boat sailors have already squirrelled away the provisions they took from the trawler. There'll be fresh fish for all of them on the way home and Krieger has got a good feeling about the journey.

"She should be sinking now," says Krieger. Stolz stands behind him and looks through his own binoculars at the *Kestrel*. It is just the two of them on the bridge but a guard stands on deck below them. Ordinarily they might make preparations for leaving but the *Kestrel* opposite them does not seem to be damaged in anyway. They will use the deck gun if needed. "What did you do in the engine room?"

"Opened the valves, she'll start to sink in a moment, I promise."

"And the bomb?"

"A stick grenade that I left just behind the hatch in the boiler. It'll go off in the next few minutes." Krieger scoffs.

"You left a man on board."

"A mistake, Captain, anyone can make one."

"I know, but there's no place for your arrogance, or the many times you've questioned my orders. I'd suggest you spend your next trip as a crewman, Stolz." The blonde man flares his nostrils. This is demotion. He will not go easily.

"To put this into perspective, Captain, it has been a successful trip so far," says Stolz. He can already taste the cognac. "We will be back in Wilhelmshaven within a few days."

"Though your cup is full, you still may spill your drink all down your front." It is bad luck to celebrate anything before it has happened, especially on a boat. Stolz has been at sea long enough to know this. Krieger takes down his binoculars and looks back at the tall man—they may have machines that can dive under the ocean but they are not more powerful than the sea herself. Stolz realises his mistake.

"If we make it home, Captain, I'd like to buy you a drink." Stolz says this to placate the gods.

"Thank you for your offer," answers Krieger. He puts his binoculars back to his eyes. He would never share a drink with Stolz, not after all this. If he did, he'd end up flattening the tall bastard after the drink got inside his head.

On the deck of the *Kestrel* opposite, the figure appears once more under the wheelhouse with his hands up in the air. He's shuffling and limping while shouting. Krieger can see he is in distress. He removes his binoculars.

"Shoot him," he calls to the sailor standing guard on the deck below them. The man reaches down to bring his rifle up, steps back and puts it to his shoulder as his eyes squint down the sights. Krieger has run out of patience. The *U-19* will sink this trawler, and whoever this man on board is, he poses a risk to the German crew. The rifleman below squeezes the trigger to shoot. The bullet pings off the wheelhouse behind the figure, and it ducks back and out of sight.

"Eyes on deck please," he says to the rifleman. "If anything moves—shoot it."

"Yes, Captain."

Just behind the hatch of the boiler in the still fierce heat of the glowing embers of coals, the stick grenade begins to melt. The wood of the handle is starting to char, and the casing inside the head is breaking down. It is taking a little longer than Stolz expected—but the explosion is getting closer.

Across the water, down in the engine room of the *Kestrel*, Tommy Woods turns the handle on the throttle to allow the steam from the boiler out into the engine. This will get the pistons going, and in turn, drive the propeller and power the ship. He listens as they begin to hum. Tommy Woods has tried to give himself up. Now he knows they'll kill him if he shows himself on board. The crew of the *Kestrel* are already rowing away.

It's the familiar feeling of being left alone because he's messed up, like always. Tommy will have to sort this out himself. There'll be no rescue. He's got the vaguest of plans. If the *Kestrel* outran that bloody U-boat before, she can do so again, and if need be, Woods will sail her all the way to the Arctic Circle just to piss them off. He's stopped the leak the German's thought they started, so he doesn't think she'll sink. He swallows. Now he's started the propellor he'll have to get to the wheelhouse. It's the only place he can steer the ship.

Woods goes up the slippery ladder from the engine room once again. He crawls through the hatch and keeps low as he sneaks across the deck. Around the corner, he sees the ladder and the open door to the wheelhouse. He will be exposed if he makes a run for it, but there's no other choice. If he is going to pilot the *Kestrel* out of this, he needs to be at the wheel. He blinks in the cold morning air. On the wind and out of sight, he can hear the shouts of the German sailors busy readying their U-boat to leave. He takes a deep breath and dashes out along the deck towards the ladder up to the wheelhouse, and on the wet floor, his wooden foot skids so that he stumbles. A bullet pings off the metal bulkhead. It would have hit him had he not slipped.

Tommy Woods grabs a rung of the ladder and hauls himself up with arms that are strong to compensate for his disability. He is quick into the wheelhouse while over the water on the *U-19*, the German rifleman lifts the bolt handle and pulls back the action to load another bullet from the magazine.

When he gets up there, Woods dips into the corner out of sight, and immediately, a bullet cracks the window and another thuds into the wall behind him. There must be a few shooters

159

on him now. A bullet whizzes in through the door which is wide open to the grey sky. Another shatters a pane of the window and splinters of glass shower the floor like ice.

Woods crouches low as he moves towards the wheel. Through gritted teeth, he reaches out and turns it full lock to bring the *Kestrel* about. More bullets shatter the rest of the glass, they ricochet off the wall into the compass and the wheel, making Woods jump back to the corner to hide. The tin cup, half full of cold tea, clatters to the ground. He puts his hands over his head in the noise. The *Kestrel* is now moving under him, but not the way he wanted. Her bow begins to turn to face the *U-19* opposite her. Woods reaches out one more time to turn the wheel in the other direction. He gets his hand to it before there's another volley of bullets and he springs back to protect himself in the corner. All he's done is straighten the *Kestrel* up.

More bullets ping through the wheelhouse window, this time at a different angle because the boat is turning. Woods presses himself into the corner as tight as he can with his head buried in his elbows.

They're an unlucky lot are the Woods family.

At least he will be with his father and his elder brother when this is all over. He'll be with them both floating down into the darkness with the spider crabs and the silver codfish, and he will know that he did the best he could, and that in the end, he was not going to give up without a fight.

Woods closes his eyes and prepares for the big boom of the deck gun that he knows is coming. The German captain will probably blow a hole in the bow, and it won't take long for the *Kestrel* to go down. Woods thinks about his sister and his mother back in Hull, how the news will affect them and how they will be forced to stay with Cousin Mathews. He hopes too, that one day, his mother will find the strength to walk out of that house and take her daughter with her.

Krieger saw the man dash out along the side of the trawler and then slip as the riflemen was about to put a bullet through him. The figure climbed up the ladder to the wheelhouse like a rat up a drainpipe, and it was only then Krieger realised the *Kestrel* was now moving and turning towards them. The man on board must have started the engine back up again. Krieger has his men fire a volley of shots at the wheelhouse but as they shoot, he sees the danger that is coming to the *U-19*. He calls for someone to man the deck gun, but there is nobody on the fore deck to do so. The crew are too victory drunk with a big sack of potatoes and the buckets of fresh fish.

The *Kestrel* is a hundred yards out from them, but the bow has turned to face the *U-19* amid the shots fired by the first sailor and others who have joined in shooting. Krieger calculates. If he jumps over the railings to the deck gun, aims it and fires, the *Kestrel* will probably still keep on going, and even if he fires a shell through the bow, it will not sink her before she hits them.

Krieger moves to the open hatch into the *U-19*, where just moments before, happy sailors carried down two buckets of fish and a big lump of cheese wrapped in a cloth. The captain is wide eyed as he bellows into the hatch. If the *Kestrel* hits them, it could be catastrophic.

"Engines forward!" and down below in the *U-19*, past the control room and the big bilge pump, smiling like it is Christmas Day, Felix himself has grabbed hold of the bottle of cognac and is taking a big glug in celebration. He hears the captain yell, and it's tinny as it carries from the world above. A crew member takes the bottle back and he scrambles aft of the *U-19* to the diesel engine that has been idle while they sink the trawler.

If Felix had been given a few minutes, he could have the engine fired up and moving, but as it is, the mechanism has been allowed to get cold. He pulls down the handle to fire up the motor and it coughs back at him in the freezing, rank smelling air. He swears under his breath and hears Krieger from high above yelling again for, "All forward". He resets the handle and the mechanism catches and spins. He pulls the choke and opens the throttle to hear the lines of pistons on both sides of the corridor room burst into action as they begin to move up and down. He grins back at the sailor, who still has the bottle of cognac in his hand, with an 'it's going to be alright' smile.

On deck, the *Kestrel* looms down from the sea at the *U-19*. She is much higher than they are in the water, heavier too. Krieger feels the engines of the *U-19* fire up from below as Felix starts them, and first mate Stolz appears on the bridge from the ladder leading down to the control room. There's a look of concern on his thin face as to why the captain has barked an order with such ferocity. Once he's on the bridge properly, he looks out to see the trawler moving towards them at speed. He gawps at the captain with wide eyes, and then glances down to the deck gun as he realises the predicament they are in. Unless they can move in the next two minutes, the *Kestrel* is going to run them over. He grits his teeth. U-boats aren't made to withstand collisions. They are precision instruments—the *SM U-18* was rammed in November last year and sunk, as was the *U-15* back in August. Stolz steps to the hatch and screams a frantic order down into the stench of the *U-19*.

"Alarm! Engines full forward! Come on!"

Riflemen shoot into the wheelhouse of the *Kestrel* where they saw the man a few minutes previous. They shatter the glass and put holes into the metal bulkheads but none of this will stop the movement of a steam trawler once it has gathered speed. Stolz yells down at Felix in the engine room once more, and his voice is hoarse and rude. Nero senses the worry and dashes the full length to the fore of the *U-19*, and the captain's bunk, where she jumps and lands on his pillow.

Felix in the engine room curses again. The machine has

stalled and he resets the handle to start it up again without quite knowing what is happening above. The pistons lose their power and stop. It will take him a few minutes to get them running again. He turns to yell back to the hatch above the control room:

"Two minutes!" It will definitely be five.

It was just as Krieger said, even though you have your cup full, it's still very possible to spill it down your front. A few minutes ago, the crew of the *U-19* were on their way home after weeks at sea. They were going to see their wives and girlfriends, sit in cozy front rooms and eat strudel that their grandmother had made. They would sleep in soft beds where they don't feel like they are drowning in their dreams. It was all hubris.

At eight knots, the *Kestrel* strikes the *U-19* on the front just fore of the deck gun that they should have fired. Because the U-boat is low in the water, the trawler runs right over her and rips open the outer tank. In slow motion almost, Krieger watches as the bow of the steam trawler carries on across her. There's the creak of iron on steel as she passes, and then a great clunk as the keel sweeps off the nose tip of the *U-19*. The bow of the U-boat dips as the *Kestrel* goes right over her. There's more scraping as the propellor under the water makes a mess of the front end, it punctures one of the torpedo tubes so that water can cascade in. It has taken just a minute for the trawler to pass over the low German U-boat, but the damage is done. The fore ballast tanks have been ripped open.

Krieger looks on in horror and feels the *U-19* sway to one side as it loses buoyancy. The sailor with a rifle on the aft deck tumbles into the water. The U-boat and the conning tower begin to lurch to one side. She is taking water. Krieger's legs flood with fear as he bellows at Stolz:

"You'll be court-marshalled for this!" It is his first instinct to blame someone else. For if the first mate had searched the ship properly, he would have found the man. If he had bothered to set a proper bomb she would already have gone under. Stolz stares back with worried, frightened eyes for he will not live to face the military court or argue his case either. The dark north waters begin to spill into the *U-19* and she creaks as she rolls over. She is languid almost as she goes onto one side and the conning tower strikes the ocean. Krieger himself tumbles overboard into the icy water with two riflemen next to him, and Stolz tries to jump back into the hatch and below.

Down in the *U-19*, confused men fall on their sides as the U-boat rotates horizontally. Water begins to piss in through the front end torpedo tubes and across the bulkhead. It runs into the berth room with the lines of beds on each side where the hammocks on hooks now sag. It seeps into the skipper's bunk where Nero whimpers, and then moves to the command room, goes past the periscope and the bilge pumps into the engine section, where Felix struggles to understand what has happened. All through this tube under the water, the crew of the *U-19* struggle against each other as they fall and tumble. The sack of potatoes they have just pilfered splits and the vegetables roll. The bottle of cognac smashes as a sailor falls, and then, as soon as they start to come to their senses, the cold ice water creeps in and floods the space so that men call out and yell. The cold of the north water kills quickly, it robs their bodies of strength and stings their minds with shock. The *U-19* creaks as she rolls into the sea.

It does not take long. All the hope that is down there, the friendship, the dreams for the future and home, the bravery and honour; the spirit and guile, all of it is snuffed out as easily as a match flame is eaten by the rain.

The crew of the *Kestrel* watch it all happen. They watch their ship pass over the U-boat bow and tear a big hole. They see the *U-19* dip forward in the crash and rock to the side with the damage.

John Grace stops rowing. George puts his hands to his forehead in worry. Big Billy swallows. Stout narrows his eyes. Cooper lifts the peak of his cap to get a better look. Young Jack blinks at the stern. Peter Everett stares down at the floor of the lifeboat; in his ears and on the wind, he can hear the call of the German men inside the U-boat, they are raw with the honesty of terror—the same yells he heard when the *HMS Pathfinder* went down. It is the horror as people are swallowed up by the sea.

Sitting at the bow of the lifeboat with his blue cat on his knee cuddled up to him, Skipper Williams grins bright and happy:

"I knew that Tommy Woods had something about him," he calls to the wind.

The *Kestrel* did not come off unscathed in the collision and as she struck the *U-19*, she too lurched to the side. The damage is minor, but the stick grenade that Stolz placed just inside the furnace door slid off the shelf and into the burning embers of the fire proper. It takes just a few seconds and, with a dull boom, it ignites and explodes in the engine room, ripping apart the boiler and pulling all the pipes and steam work off the wall in the fury and noise. The *Kestrel* cockles backwards and a great hole opens at the side of the engine room where water pours in.

On the ocean, Skipper Williams turns to John Grace and Billy at the oars:

"Row strong lads," he orders. When a boat even the size of the *Kestrel* goes down, it will pull anything in the immediate area down with it—that will include the lifeboat if they are not far enough away.

The two men fall to rowing and Skipper Williams leans forward to watch the catastrophe unfold. Both vessels are going down with all hands. In the water next to the *U-19*, he can see heads bobbing behind the waves that are there one second, and then gone the next. The *U-19* is going under bow first as it fills on the inside; water seeps in through the conning tower and the front end as it begins to be swallowed by the sea. Behind, the *Kestrel* is sinking backwards, the water eats up her rear end and as she slips under, the whole of the vessel tips up vertically. Williams watches the wheelhouse disappear under the north water followed by the trawl winch and then the bow. There's a gurgling noise from the ocean as it swallows them up whole.

It has happened so quickly, and now the vessels are gone; there is just the silent indifference of the waves. The lifeboat rocks on the sea and the men stop rowing. Where once there was a trawler and a U-boat, there is nothing at all but the dark ocean and the waves that never stop. Skipper Williams turns to his men to see their faces washed out and hollow. The old man is not surprised—the sea's cruelty is nothing new to him.

There is no celebration here.

The crew on board the *U-19* were not enemies. Somewhere over the great oceans and in the cities south of them, men who will never sail out on the frozen seas order their sailors and navy to go where they would not dare.

CHAPTER SEVENTEEN

Morning turns to noon and the sky darkens. The crew of the *Kestrel* drift. There is no point rowing because there is nowhere to row to. In every direction there is nothing but the flat horizon. The lifeboat has supplies. There are blankets and perhaps a few days' worth of food in tin cans. A light gale picks up from the east, and the men huddle down under the blankets and their coats. They get as low as they can to the lifeboat so they can stay out of the wind.

Skipper Williams keeps watch with his back to the bow of the ship and his leather face looking out at the water behind them. He is sorry they lost Woods. Perhaps he's getting old, for it is the first time he's felt that tinge of sadness and remorse inside his stomach since he lost his uncle. He thought at his age he was immune to it. The cat squirms on his knee. He thinks about home and his big house on the Boulevard with his nagging daughter. It has been good to be back out at sea with rough men rather than a life of ease in a gilded cage. He licks his lips. Looking up at him from just under his blanket where he lies on the floor of the lifeboat, is Young Jack. The lad has aged with these experiences.

"Are we going to die?" he whispers to the skipper. He should really know better than to ask this kind of a question to a man such as Williams.

"I should think so," he answers. His old eyes blink, they are red and pale around the edges. "It won't do you any good to go worrying about it though, Young Jack, there's nothing you can do." These were meant to be words of comfort, but the lad just covers his face with his blanket. Williams was about his age when he lost his uncle.

At the port side of the lifeboat and curled up on his side, asleep, is Stout. He breathes deep with his coat over him, and there is nothing at all in his dreams but the sweet sensation of the lifeboat rocking on the waves below.

Peter Everett sits next to John Grace and now the *U-19* is sunk, he feels his left leg beginning to shake very slightly. This is how it started after he'd been dragged from the wreckage of the *HMS Pathfinder*; he knows that in a day he will be back to the shaking mess he was previous. He swallows. His throat is raw. It would have been better if they had drowned.

John Grace can't sit with his knees up to his chest anymore, his body is too stiff and old. His cold blue eyes look out across the freezing noon waters.

"It would be better if we'd been drowned," he says, echoing Peter Everett's thoughts.

"It would have been quicker at least," says Peter Everett. "We'll drift like this till a big wave turns us over."

George begins his next coughing fit from where he sits at the stern. He leans forwards and puts his head over the side of the boat towards the water, his face goes red as he hacks, with his whole body tensing at every bitter cough that rasps at his lungs. It takes a few minutes and the rest of the crew listen to him struggle. They feel his pain. George wipes his mouth on his sleeve and there is blood all over the material.

"Even if we get back to Hull," says Skipper Williams to George, "you'll be dead before the end of the month." George grins back at him because he knows this might be true. He has learned the fatalism of these fishermen and he likes it; he has taken also some of the darkness of this north water into him.

"Not a word of this, by the way, lads." It's Skipper Williams speaking again. "You who haven't been trawling before, if we do make it back, you're not to go shouting your mouth off about what happened here." He looks at George and then Billy, at John Grace too. He can imagine them pissed up in some pub and describing how the *Kestrel* tore open the bow of the *U-19*, then how they heard the cries of the drowning German sailors. This is not what Hull fishermen do, for boasting is the worst of many crimes on the sea. Shout loud enough about yourself and the ocean will want you. "What happened here stays out here, not a bloody soul would believe you anyway. I don't believe it myself, and if you repeat it, I'll say you're a liar." He looks to the ashen faces of the crew to make sure they've heard him. He has never given such orders to be quiet before. He's never needed to. The words sink into the men on board the lifeboat.

"There'll be a few drinks when I get back," says George. He has returned to sit inside the boat after his coughing fit, and his lips are pale with his skin tight against his cheekbones. Skipper Williams scoffs at this optimism.

"I know where I'm going," says Big Billy. He has been largely quiet since they began to drift and the scar on his head is dry.

"Tell us where, Billy," says George.

"Tyne Street."

"Where's that?"

"I don't right know," says the big man.

"It's off Hessle Road," this is Cooper sitting next to him.

"What's there?"

"It's where Woods lived." The eyes of the crew fall on Billy when he mentions this name.

"What for, lad?" this is Skipper Williams with his face a frown.

"He told me and George, he said that he lived with his cousin, and that he was a right horrible bastard to him and his mam and sister." Billy looks across at the ocean but he is not looking anywhere, in his mind he is walking down an unknown street off Hessle Road looking for the house that Woods described to him a few days before.

"I shall go to the front door," he continues, "and thump on the wood with my hand. I'll step back and I'll wait. When the door opens, I'll announce that I'm here to see that fat bastard Mathews, and the moment he gets to the door, I'll pull him out by the scruff of his neck into the street and I'll clobber him one around the head. I shall tell him that he deserves the hiding he's about to get for the things he did to my pal, Woods, and his mother and sister." Billy's eyes are moist as he says this, and the men in the lifeboat of the *Kestrel* around him look on with nodding heads, for Woods was a good lad—as good as they come even.

"You're a fine fellow, Big Billy," says Skipper Williams from the bow.

It is perhaps the only nice thing he has said in sixty years.

The afternoon is deathly cold and the air begins to freeze around the men. Peter Everett's shaking is returning but the cold is hampering his body's efforts, so he can only chatter his teeth with the blanket over his head. Darkness creeps upon the lifeboat in the late afternoon and smothers all sound and light and hope.

She's a fishing ship out of Dundee, a steam trawler bigger than the *Kestrel* called the Terrier. They spot the lifeboat through the fog on their way out to the fishing grounds, and when they get to the rowboat in the first light of morning, the men are nearly frozen solid. It takes a while to get them on board and when they do, the Scottish trawler men set them in the mess room on the Terrier and feed them sweet, hot tea.

The men explain they were sunk by a U-boat. They don't say anything more, the crew of the Terrier don't expect anything else, they're lads from Hull. They won't tell you the time if they don't know you.

The big one with blonde hair who calls himself Billy is okay to work, so is the kid with his rabbit teeth. The one with the filthy clothes who stinks is good enough to haul nets as well, and the cook went to washing pots in the galley. Not the others. One of them suffers from coughing fits, another one who said he was the engineer shakes all the time, another fat one has caught a chill. The old man with the white tash says he was the skipper of the *Kestrel* and he knows where to catch alright. Just off the north coast of Scotland they fish for two

170

days till they've filled the fishroom.

The Hull men keep one eye on the horizon while they fish but otherwise, they stick to the same story—that they were put adrift by a German U-boat. They shrug their shoulders at the number of the vessel written on the front although they all know it was the *U-19*. Like Williams ordered, there's no need to tell the story of what happened. No one would believe it anyway.

It is three days till they get back to Dundee. The Humber Steam Trawling Company has an office on the docks there, and it is a formality to get the crew of the *Kestrel* transferred back down to Hull on a carrier. Before the week is out, the eight men left of the crew are delivered down the coast, stopping at Middlesbrough for a time and then going down to Hull.

The merchant ship doesn't take them to St Andrews Dock where they started out—that's mostly for fish and so, on 14th March 1915, in the early evening darkness, they land at Junction Dock in the middle of town. Under the statue of William Wilberforce, they walk down the gangplank with the smell and the lights of the city in front of them.

They have not been told so, but it is common practice that none of the men will be paid for their time on board the *Kestrel* because it has been lost. In fact, they could be in debt to the company for their trip back to Hull. Skipper Williams will be required to explain the events to his superiors at the Hull Steam Trawling Company. It will probably be Mr Keel who hears this. They may fine him or revoke his skipper's ticket for a few months but Williams isn't planning on sailing again, so he won't give a toss.

He has given the crew one last order to follow when they disembark the ship. It is an invitation to his house on the Boulevard—number one hundred and sixty five. John Grace whispered to the men that since they were landing at six, they should make it to the skipper's house for seven. It's a half hour walk from town, if you know where you are going.

George Jackson stands on the dock and looks over at the City Hall in the light from the gas streetlamps. A horse and carriage draw past him. There's the shout of a newspaper seller down Saville Street and the familiar smells of tobacco smoke, horse manure and the distant whiff of coal. It does not seem real that he and Sam queued up at the very building he looks upon some three weeks ago to join the war effort. Here George stands once again. In his thick jumper and braces over both shoulders to keep his trousers up, he looks more a sailor than a country lad from Cottingham.

Big Billy appears behind him. He's wearing a woolly hat and his straight blonde hair peeps out from underneath the knit work.

"I'm going," he says in his deep voice.

"We're to meet the skipper at his house."

"Not me," says Billy. George knows his plans. Fat Stout steps to the side of them both, he is also aware of where Billy is planning on going.

"It's on the way to Tyne Street," he says through a grin. The idea that someone is going to get their head smashed in excites him.

"You know the way, do you?" he asks. Stout nods.

"What about the skipper?" asks George.

"He won't be walking," says Stout. "He'll have gone off in a carriage with John Grace and the engineer. Skippers don't have to walk in this city like us rats." Now Stout is back on home ground, he can be a smart arse like he tried to be at sea.

Cooper joins them with Young Jack next to him and the five of them begin the journey down the side of the dock, over monument bridge and down past City Hall. There are no kit bags over their shoulders and no smiles either. A bright tram that they cannot afford to catch whizzes past on its tracks with the bells jingling as it goes down Carr Lane towards Anlaby

Road. Though it's dark and cold in the city, it feels alive with life and activity after where these men have been. The wind is sharp, but nothing like what they have endured.

The Boulevard is a posh street. It's long and wide flanked by trees in front of big, terraced houses and at half an hours' walk from St Andrews fish dock, it is here where you may find professionals of moderate to good money such as school masters, medical doctors, lawyers of sorts and ship's captains. Trawler skippers can be as rough as the North Sea but they're also very well paid and their money allows them to set up in places such as the Boulevard. Skipper Williams has commanded hundreds of fishing trips and so his wealth will be considerable. There's a lad in a cap pushing an empty handcart, a motor car eases past them and in the cold March evening, the working crew of the *Kestrel* feel out of place between these well-kept buildings and tidy scrubbed front steps.

Stout leads the way past an ornate fountain in the centre where two streets meet to form a roundabout. The water is turned off now because it's too cold, but a circle of mermen with shell trumpets to their mouths sit below another ring of porcelain flamingos. George wrinkles his nose as they walk by. It is the pomp of the rich.

At one hundred and sixty-five the group stop. It is noticeably bigger than the rest and next to a dispensary chemist that is now closed. They wait at the front door and are nervous about who should knock. Cooper feels so out of place, he thinks about removing his mucky cap. It's not like George Jackson has time to waste, so he steps through and goes down the path to the front door where a lamp illuminates the well-presented hall. He's about to take the big door knocker in his hand, when he hears the clatter of hooves down the street, and a carriage pulls up outside the house.

On the cab is a gruff looking driver with a cloth cap and a

big moustache. He knocks on his seat with the handle of his whip to indicate to his passengers that they have arrived.

The door to the cab opens outwards and the little figure of Skipper Williams steps into the street with his white moustache and big rolled-necked jumper. Following is John Grace and then Peter Everett. The engineer's head is already shaking like it did when he first got on board the *Kestrel* and his eyes look misty. There's the waft of strong drink on the breath of the three of them.

"I thought you'd have got here before us, Skipper." This is Stout.

"We went for a drink first," answers Williams. Over his shoulder is the blue cat that travelled with him on the *Kestrel*. The old man's nose is red from the booze. He strides down the path to one hundred and sixty-five the Boulevard and throws open the door. The lights are on in the hall. He calls in a loud voice into the big house:

"Vanessa, I have returned from the sea and I have guests." He walks down the hall barking more orders as he goes, as if they have been expecting him at any moment. "I shall be upstairs in my drawing room and I will need the fire lit at once." From around the bottom of the staircase appears a brown, short haired lass in a long dress with high collars. She has pinched painted red lips and looks shocked.

"Father!" she exclaims. She is clearly a woman of her father's means.

"Did you hear what I said?" asks Skipper Williams. She nods. There is no warm greeting from either of them. She catches her breath.

"The fire is lit in the front room, Father, if you would like to take your guests there."

"I said I would take them upstairs in my drawing room, Vanessa." She looks past him to the men waiting outside.

"But their boots on the carpets, Father? Why the mess they'll bring in."

"You shall watch the way you speak to me, Miss. This is my house, and if I should wish to muddy up the bloody carpets then I shall." It's strange for the crew of the *Kestrel* to hear him annoyed at something so small, and it reveals a little of his life here in this posh house on the Boulevard. Out at sea he may be a skipper, but here, he is perhaps more an annoyance than a commander.

"I'll get a lamp from the kitchen, Father."

The seven men of the *Kestrel* stand in the hall of the three storey house. The skipper has already disappeared up the stairs with his daughter to attend to the lights. The smell and the warmth of the building are foreign to these men who have been at sea, and they huddle close as they stand there. Peter Everett has begun to shake more noticeably now he is getting warmer. John Grace smells of the drink. Big Billy takes off his woolly hat but Cooper does not remove his. Presently, there's a call from above and they follow John Grace up the stairs one by one.

This does not happen. Skippers do not invite their crews to their houses; they may buy them a drink, and if they pass each other in the street there will be a curt nod but that is all. John Grace leads the way up and onto the landing into the backroom. He can see that Williams has it as some sort of library, and huge bookcases fill the far wall. There's a red leather chesterfield armchair in the corner below an ornate lamp on the table.

Williams stands next to the windowsill, and gently takes the blue cat from his shoulders to set it down on a round, red velvet bed on a little table. The cat oozes onto the material, pads around for a moment, and then sits upright with an air of arrogance. It's as if she has not been out over the great North Sea and south of Iceland, as if she has not been forced adrift in a lifeboat and then watched as both her trawler and a U-boat sank into the aloof ocean until there was nothing left

175

but the silence of the waves. The cat curls up with her big tail around her.

"Step through boys," calls Skipper Williams, "you won't be here for long." The men of the *Kestrel* file into the drawing room one by one and stand in a line next to the bookcase. "You can take off your bloody hat though, Cooper, we're not on a trawler now." Cooper struggles with this, and his hand goes to the peak of his filthy cap in worry that he will have to reveal himself to the others. He swallows. There is no getting out of it, so he removes the coal stained paperboy hat from his head to reveal short copper hair—it's not the colour or the style that Cooper is worried about, more the eyes and the shape of the head that could reveal who he has tried to get away from being all these years. In the dim light from the lamp in the drawing room, none of these trawlermen notice.

The skipper's daughter, Vanessa, enters the room carrying a tray full of wine glasses. Each one is lipped with a band of small crosscut diamonds and is filled with a tea coloured liquid, it's whiskey. Only perhaps Peter Everett would have drunk from something like this before. Skipper Williams settles himself down in the red leather chesterfield armchair, and like the cat, it does not seem as if he has been on a great adventure. Vanessa walks down the line of men and they each take a glass, even Jack. She steps back with the empty tray in her hand.

"You can leave us now, lass," says Williams. She gives him a sour look and backs out of the drawing room closing the door. The men of the *Kestrel* stand in silence with the sound of a grandfather clock behind them ticking loudly. Williams leans over to the bookcase next to him and removes three big books from the shelf to reveal the face of a metal safe. He concentrates on the dial with his shaky hands, turning first to this number and then to that, as he enters the combination. It opens with a click and he reaches in to grab a tall pile of notes. He closes the door and sets the pile on the table next to him.

"Come over here Young Jack," he calls. The lad steps

forwards with the glass of brown liquid trembling in his hand. "I'll have that drink, kid, it'll not do you any good." Jack hands the old man the glass. "Now, I want you to take seven twenty-pound notes from that pile there, one for each man in this room. One of them is yours." Jack blinks at him. This is a lot of money, more than any one of them could have expected to earn on board the *Kestrel* in one trip. It is worth perhaps a year of catches. Jack sets to with the job, gingerly he counts out seven of the big notes and sees written on each one in big letters, the pound symbol, the two and the zero. It is all he knows how to read. He walks to the end of the line and passes one to each man.

Stout is first, and he snatches the paper in his fat fingers, folds it and slips it in the side pocket of his trousers. Peter Everett is struggling to hold is glass level because he is shaking so much. He takes the cash. Big Billy takes his share with a concerned frown as to the catch. George says 'thank you' to the lad. Cooper collects his money and Jack looks him in the eyes for the first time. John Grace nods in thanks, and he takes the twenty pound note in his big hands. The last note belongs to Young Jack.

"I'm not one for speeches," says Skipper Williams as he raises the glass of whiskey, "but a man who works hard deserves to be paid." He tips the glass down his throat in one go, and the men of the *Kestrel* do the same.

The money is considerable.

It will pay off John Grace's debt. It will mean Stout can visit that bawdy house next to the Old Grey Mare pub in town. Big Billy does not quite know what this amount of money means, certainly Jack doesn't either. For Cooper, he will have to hide it away somewhere because it might be more trouble than it's worth. George will give it to his mother; it will give her security while he and Sam are away at war. Peter Everett blinks down at the note in his shaking hand, it does not mean anything to him—he will go back to his wife and his house in

Bridlington, but she will ask him to leave again, while he shakes like he does. She cannot stand him in the house.

"You can leave your glasses with Vanessa on the way out." This is the skipper telling them to piss off.

"I'd like to say something on behalf of the lads," says John Grace.

"No need for all that shite," says the old man, "I've done well out of the sea over these years." John Grace nods. He will go directly to the Black Boy pub on Main Street, to the upstairs room where they play cards when the pub is closed, and he'll pay back what he owes. Maybe he'll have a drink, his luck could be in, he could even play a hand or too with the money he has left.

At the front door, as quickly as they came together, the crew disperse. John Grace is eager to be off one way, he and Peter Everett walk back towards town, Stout heads off into the darkness without any clever talk because he has so much money in his pocket. Young Jack and Cooper are going in the opposite direction, Jack's mother lives on Spring Bank just over a mile away and Cooper doesn't have anywhere else to go, so they'll walk together.

It leaves George and Big Billy standing in the cold wind looking in the direction of Hessle Road. It's just past eight on a Tuesday evening in March. They both know what's to be done.

"I'll ask someone which street it is when we get nearer," says Billy. George nods and they fall into step with each other towards Hessle Road. It takes a couple of minutes to reach the main street. They pass a group of soldiers in uniform, a horse and cart carrying beer barrels, two coppers with wide moustaches and shiny buttons on their jackets, and a gentleman in a suit. Even though it's evening, there's still a buzz about the place. It's nothing at all like the sleepy villages these men come from, and far removed from the remote wastes of the north waters.

On the corner of West Dock Ave stands an alehouse called the Star and Garter. There's piano music coming from within the front door and the sound of men chatting. It looks warm on such a cold night. George grabs Billy's jacket sleeve to stop him. The big man turns.

"I think we should have a pint," says George.

"We will," says Billy, "after I get to Tyne Street and do what I said I would."

"Remember that pub Woods told us about. This is it. The Star and Garter."

"What about his cousin?"

"He'll probably be in bed, Billy. It'd be much better if me and you went into the alehouse here, had a good sit down, a natter, and then a stopover in one of the rooms upstairs if they have them." The idea sounds appealing. Billy looks across at the pub. He can hear shouting, laughter and a woman shrieking as if she's drunk.

"It's a trawlerman's pub," he says as if that means it's not for them.

"We're trawlermen, Billy, look at the way we're dressed. I've never had twenty quid before and I've never ordered a whiskey in a pub." Billy looks down on this man he has only known a few weeks, but who he now considers a friend. He sees the hollow cheeks and red eyes. Like Skipper Williams said, George doesn't look like he has long left. "We can go on up to Tyne Street in the morning," continues George. "We'll batter him then, that way, all the neighbours will get to see as well." This makes sense. "It'll be easier to find in the daytime too." Billy looks over to the lights of the pub and now hears a chorus of singing. It does sound like a good place. "We'll have a drink for Woods, that's what he'd want."

"Maybe you're right," says Billy.

"But no fighting till tomorrow." The big blonde man grins and shows the gap between his two front teeth.

It is a good night.

Billy insists on paying for everything. The piano player tries to go home at ten but Billy gives him half a crown to keep on. There's a steam trawler that docked in the afternoon called the *Outland*, and the crew caught heavy. Fish is a good price now the war is on and so they got paid well. They're hard men who drink deep and know the value of the time they have. They have heard of the *Kestrel* too, and Skipper Williams and how it was sunk by a German U-boat. This makes George and Big Billy welcome friends.

They sing at the top of their voices next to the piano, squabble over the privilege of paying for the drinks, arm wrestle on the tables in just their vest tops way after closing time when the landlord has locked the doors. And when it is all done, the men of the *Outland* stumble home and the landlord invites Billy and George Jackson into the back bedroom upstairs where they can pass out on the double bed. He's already made more from both of them than he feels happy with. Trawlermen are the life of this street so they have to be looked after.

It is eight o'clock in the morning. Big Billy still has his boots on under the blanket on the double bed. He opens his eyes and his head throbs from the drink. For a moment he wonders where he is and then the memory comes to him through the fog and smoke from the night before—the singing, the arm wrestling, the deep and serious conversation, and he smiles at it.

He sits up and expects to see George Jackson next to him, but there's only a neatly folded blanket where the man should be. Billy manages to get up and washes his face in the sink as he thinks about the night before. He has been offered a job aboard the *Outland*, which sails in three days' time and he'll take it. He smiles again as he puts on his heavy jacket.

Wherever George has got to, Billy has an errand to run,

and he doesn't want to put it off any longer.

The bar room of the pub looks different and dreary in the daytime. There's a young lass sweeping up and the landlady is pulling stale beer through one of the hand pumps. Billy gives her a nod.

"How much do I owe you?" He means for the room.

"You paid me last night, you big lug," she says. Billy doesn't remember but he likes the way she insults him.

"Where's my mate?"

"He left about an hour ago, said not to wake you."

"Where did he go?"

"Cottingham, I think." The landlady fills a pint glass with water from a bottle and puts it on the bar for Billy. He swallows it down in two gulps.

"You look like shite," she says.

"Which way is Tyne Street?" he asks.

"Just down Dee Street here and turn left. Visiting family, are you?"

"Something like that," he answers.

In the new, grey light of the morning, Hessle Road is busier than the night before. Men on black bicycles with flat caps ride to factory jobs. There's a group of school kids carrying satchels on the other side of the road. Shop keepers are unlocking their front doors and pulling up the blinds for the day ahead.

Billy feels out of place as he crosses the road to Dee Street. He clumps his way past the terraced houses. The windows are covered by net curtains and the dark passageways between some of them look cold. There are two women nattering outside their front door who look at him with disdain, people don't like strangers round here. He passes cramped alleys and snickets, there's the smell of grease from bacon cooking and also the stink from the outbuildings at the back of these houses huddled together. Billy keeps on till he sees a sign stuck to a house wall that he thinks reads Tyne Street. This is it.

He walks halfway down the rows of houses on each side and stops a man with a cloth cap walking the other way.

"I'm looking for a family named Woods," asks Billy. He doesn't mean to sound unfriendly. The man narrows his eyes.

"What do you want them for?" People defend each other along this street.

"I was a mate of Woods, Tommy Woods." The man's expression changes. You hear news quickly around here.

"They're on Laura Grove, on your left. It's the corner house." Billy listens. "He was a good lad," says the man with the cloth cap. Billy agrees.

He finds Laura Grove on the right, and there's the corner house. It's the first in a little alley of buildings facing each other. Billy stops. He takes a deep breath as he thinks about Tommy Woods with his knackered foot and limp. He thinks of the open sky while they were on the trawler and feels the *Kestrel* rocking under his feet. He remembers that inside this house is a bully and thug who deserves the kicking he is about to serve up.

There's more. Billy stands looking at the little house with a tiny paved front garden for a moment. Some three weeks before, in a drunken fight with his father, he murdered the old bastard. So, if he batters this man and gets caught for it, the coppers will soon find out he's a wanted man back in Beverley. Woods would counsel him not to do this, he would tell him to use what little sense he has to walk away, hide up for three days and then set sail on the *Outland* trawler.

Woods was smart like that.

Billy isn't.

He'll have to get this job done because, if he doesn't, who else will? Then another bully will get away unpunished, just like the schoolteachers who mock their students, like the coppers who lock up innocent men, like the army sergeants who order their soldiers into the battle at the front, and their superiors sitting in oak panel rooms smoking cigars with glasses of brandy, who order their soldiers to hunt other men and die in the process.

Billy walks down the little path and thumps on the door with the fat of his hand then steps back. It opens quickly to a front room and a mousey looking woman with short brown hair and a worried face. Behind her, laid prone on the floor is the shape of a big man with a fat gut. He looks in a state. Next to him stands a young girl of perhaps fourteen, Billy can see Woods in her frightened features, this will be his sister.

"What do you want?" asks the woman. Her voice is sharp.

"A fella called Mathews," says Billy. The woman scowls.

"What do you want with him?"

"He's got it coming, lass, and you'll have it coming to, if you don't get out of my way." Billy has never hit a woman before and is just saying it to sound more fearful.

"You're too bloody late," she barks. "Someone was here not half an hour ago, a thin fella. See," she points over to the man lying on the floor of the terraced house—there's light groaning coming from his chest. "He threatened him first," continues the woman, "he said that my Tommy told him everything on that trawler before he died. He told him all the things Mathews had done to me and his sister, and then he slapped him up and down the room. He left him on the floor, where he is now, and then he told me he'd sailed with our Tommy on the *Kestrel* and that he was sunk by a German U-boat." The pitch of the woman's voice is getting higher as she becomes more hysterical. "It was just last night I found out I'd lost my boy, and now this happens."

Billy's fists drop to his side. He reaches into his jacket pocket and pulls out the notes and coins left from their drinking session the night before; there will be more than sixteen or seventeen quid. This was part of his plan as well. He was to batter Mathews, then give all the money to the mam and sister and tell them they don't have to live there anymore. He takes the cash and coins out in a big fistful and holds it to the woman. She shakes her head.

"You're too late for that as well," in her hand is a twenty-pound note just like the ones that Skipper Williams gave out the night before.

"Had a cough, did he?" asks Billy.

"Aye, he coughed his lungs up on the step before he left."
Billy nods.

It was George Jackson.

Billy has been outclassed at his own game.

EPILOGUE

It's nine o'clock in the morning.

This is the City Hall building on Queen Victoria Square. George walked here from Hessle Road and has been waiting at the front doors of the recruitment office for the last twenty minutes. He is dressed yet in the clothes he got from working on the *Kestrel*, the boots and jumper with braces over his shoulders. His eyes are red and the knuckles on his right hand hurt from where he belted the man on Tyne Street. He has a hangover from the drinking the night before.

George is not proud of what he did to Mathews, but it was either that or Big Billy did it, and then the fat man would be knocked out cold or dead. Big Billy would be in jail as well, then he'd be hanged. Like he's learned, George knows how to be a big brother—he's been doing it all his life. He doesn't need the money Skipper Williams gave him either, not where he is going. He's glad he gave it away.

A queue is forming behind him outside the recruitment office. They are men much as before, those eager to fight the Kaiser out in France to defend their country, those keen to show how brave they are and also, those who have been forced into it. George is not the same man as he was three weeks ago when he came here with Sam. He has stolen some of the darkness from the north waters and he carries it with him. It's what makes him strong.

The City Hall opens, and as before, the men feed in through the huge double doors and then up the main staircase. On the walls are flags and posters with Lord Kitchener's face and his finger pointing outwards. At the top of the stairs a soldier in uniform directs six men to the right and six men to the left. This time George is the first. He goes right just as he did before with five other men.

Behind screens, the men remove all their clothes down to their pants. They then form a line in front of a man dressed in a white coat with an angular face and a moustache, it is the same army doctor as before, and he still gets a penny for everyman that he examines. George is first in line.

The doctor smells of cigar smoke and aftershave. He notes down George's height using the stadiometer, asks him to step forward, cups his balls and tells him to cough. George puts his hand to his mouth and does so. It hurts. The doctor with a moustache does not show any emotion. This is just a job, and these people may as well be lumps of meat hanging in the butcher's shop window. The end of the stethoscope is cold on George's chest, he coughs again, and the doctor listens to both sides then his back. He looks at George's hands too and at the end of his fingers.

"How old are you?" asks the doctor. The same question.

"Eighteen," he answers. The doctor writes notes on a clipboard. He tells George he can get dressed and moves onto the next man.

They are told to go back and wait in the corridor outside, and after a few minutes, the five other men are called through to the office leaving George alone in the corridor. In another minute, he is called back into the examination room. Last time there were others with him, this time he is alone. Here is where the army doctor will tell him that he is not fit to join up and fight or go to the front. The men have already left through another door because they will be required to swear an oath to the king. George is conscious of the answer he requires from this medical man. Someone will have to look after Sam.

The doctor picks up the clipboard where he made notes about George earlier. He looks them over through his half-moon glasses.

"You've got a bad chest," says the doctor. "I think you'd be better visiting the infirmary rather than going off to the front."

"I know," answers George. The doctor takes a smooth breath in through his nose as he examines this serious man dressed in trawlerman's braces over a thick woollen jumper.

"It would be good if you could make a decision that I'm happy with, doctor," continues George. "My brother has already signed up and I need to be with him." There's steel in the man's voice. The doctor furrows his brow as he considers his next move. He is not used to being told what to do, but by the clothes and the smell of this thin man he concludes that he'll be one of those rough fishermen, and potentially dangerous.

"What if I don't make a decision you're happy with? Are you a medical man?" asks the doctor. It's meant to be rhetorical. George borrows a line from Big Billy:

"If I don't get the answer I want, doctor. I'll use your head to put a big hole through this office door." George is not kidding. The doctor grins as if he is used to this kind of banter fresh off the dock, but he isn't. He can pretend that George is joking when it is clear the thin man is deadly serious. What does the doctor care anyway? He gets a penny for everyman he sees regardless of if they're fit or not.

"You won't last long, son," he says.

George fixes the doctor with a cold stare.

"I'll last long enough," he answers.

#

Sign up for the Chris Speck newsletter here:
https://www.chrisspeck.co.uk/
Follow on insta here:
https://www.instagram.com/chris.speck.writer
For more of Chris Speck's books visit the Amazon page
here: https://amzn.to/3Nq27eQ

A Hull whaling novel will be out in 2027.